John Christophe was adopted, sent to a private school staffed by ex-military; character building, then Grammar, then out to work. He discovered his adoption only in his 40s. A pivotal and haunting moment.

His natural talent for drawing, his acute sense of right and wrong and his desire for knowledge have moulded his life. He studied for a PhD, was headhunted to lead several international design projects, can fly a light aircraft, pilot a boat, ride a motorcycle and loves classic cars. Should have kept some.

But his real passions are his wife, family, wildlife, nature and the environment.

Dedicated to my wife for her enduring patience and belief in me.

JOHN CHRISTOPHE

297

AUSTIN MACAULEY PUBLISHERS®

LONDON * CAMBRIDGE * NEW YORK * SHARJAH

A CIP catalogue record for this title is available from the British Library.

ISBN 9781035862900 (Paperback)
ISBN 9781035862917 (ePub e-book)

www.austinmacauley.com

First Published 2024
Austin Macauley Publishers Ltd®
1 Canada Square
Canary Wharf
London
E14 5AA

297

The space is all white; there are no walls, no edges, no noise. An attractive, funny, complicated and intriguing female human figure is seated at a desk; there is a dog by her feet, a very large malamute called Meeka. She, Gabriella, is wearing a pair of mauve skates upon which, every now and again, she gets up and puts a sheet of paper into a large black globe floating near the desk or perhaps it's far away. The globe absorbs the note. She pours a cup of coffee from a battered old coffeepot that sits on the desk.

She is recording all the events, it's not a diary, it's a…well, perhaps it's a prediction. There are pages upon pages of drawings and calculations, most of which she has distorted with a colour wash, she might change that; also, people, places, galaxies, entities and the timeline…It's necessary.

It's written from a point in Earth's future (2051) and looks back at the events which shaped humanity into something else and in which she played her part. The story is not yet finished or perhaps it is. It rather depends on your perspective and where you are. There is a jumble to the record, a random chaos that amuses Meeka who is now more logical than Gabriella, despite her colossal intelligence, ever was. The sequence of the record does not matter as the globe puts everything in order. Perhaps the events change as the globe orders them. Gabriella offers another sheet to the globe which instantly absorbs it. Briefly, a star date appears on the globe.

Gabriella is not disturbed by the globe. She and it and Meeka are here temporarily, for the sake of the record.

She is writing it in French, just for fun. Meeka prefers the language of the others in the story, which is how he regards it, particularly those who communicate in Japanese but really enjoys best the conversations with Henry as in these, he does not need to speak at all. Thought transfer is instantaneous.

Meeka is content with the story, especially the parts that feature him and he is looking forward to the next adventure.

Let it unfold

A History of the Future
Translated from the French.
Beginning 20 10 2021…numerically interesting

Gabriella's Record

Record 1
2030
The Beginning
Indicators of future problems. 30 years ago

1. Phones seem to be welded to people's ears. A study about the new words circulating, mainly among young people, reveals the reasons were COVID-19 and their resultant isolation and the use of texts as a major communication platform on social media to mitigate their loss. With this came the alienation of the older population and a societal shift towards an even more selfish one.
2. Avatars, motion graphics and the distortion of reality meant that self-image dislikes could be simply changed with the click of an APP. Real events could be given an alternative reality, For example, Donald Trump's 'Deep fake'.
3. In advertising and media marketing, the new family is composed of ethnically mixed people and robots!
4. Almost all daily activities, facilities and services are now automatic or accessible only by automated systems. The others, for example, the doctor, shopping, are almost so.
5. No APP. No service. Bugger you!

It was clear that a method to communicate with AI was essential if humanity was to survive beyond the next self-centred generation.

Gabriella skates for a coffee, followed by Meeka. The globe seems further away, temporarily. She scribbles another page.

Start note:

Since 2028 and the arrival of non-organic aliens and their first-choice communication with AI, humanity has been on the back foot.

The obvious characteristics of extra-terrestrials, their size and their colour make them very easy to identify but the problem is their effect on Earth's technological and ecological systems. They seem to ignore humans and because of their energy shield, we do not seem able to access them.

End note

2031 The number of aliens is estimated at 2 billion and continues to grow. Meanwhile, the human population is now estimated at 4.8 billion and falling.

2032
Research Complex 'Endgame' in Hawaii

Since Pearl Harbour, 7 December 1941 about 07.55 hours, the United States had egg on its face and a disaster on its hands. As a consequence, since then it has developed further bases on the islands.

What was not known was that since 1951, construction had begun on a secret basement to accommodate an intelligence gathering unit.

Over time, it has been enlarged, section by section in response to current crises or missions but also by crises both true and imagined.

By 2030, the base had increased dramatically by extending eastward under Route 99 and the H2 road to the golf course and the mountain range.

In 2021, there are 13 in total, of which Wheeler is number 5 and number 11 is the Triple Medical Centre. The facilities are:

1. Fort Shafter Military Base/Schofield Barracks
2. Hickham
3. Common Base Pearl Harbour Hickham
4. Marine Core Hawaii Base
5. Wheeler Army Aerodrome
6. Fort Shaftner
7. Camp Smith
8. AFB Bellows
9. 297th ATCS

10. USCG Air Station
11. Tripler Army Medical Centre
12. Kunia Field Station
13. Pohakulao Training Area

At that time (2021), 'Endgame' was still a secret. There were five complexes.
By 2030, the secret complex under Wheeler would occupy 30 acres and include 20 sections. The excavated materials had been used to create landscaping east of Highway 2 (H2)

The Complex

1   (The most secret) alien intelligence, gathering and analysis (AIRC)
2   Alien weapons systems, research and development (R&D)
3   Transdimensional research. (RT) (the second-most secret)
4   Communications (CMM), with the world
5   Cybernetics Research and Development (CRD)
6   Nuclear Park Systems (SN)
7   Nuclear power plant, small units developed by Rolls Royce from 2021–29, and waste disposal (NPP)
8   Neighbourhood accommodation (QA)
9   Central Administration Centre (CA)
10 Cafes and restaurants (CR)
11 Kitchens (C 1-5)
12 Laundry (B1-2)
13 Dental (D1)
14 Prayer (P1-5)
15 Decontamination (FOM) do or die
16 Vehicle Traffic Ring (VAC)
17 Traffic on foot only (CPS) get out!
18 R&R (R&R)
19 Doctors and the hospital (H)
20 Expansion ring and subsequent developments (ERD)

The Architectural Form:

A series of hubs on a radial plan with storage, equipment and utility flows constructed by cutting and covering, forming shallow ovals and tunnel sections like those used in the construction of the Cross Rail tube in the UK and all in secret.

Each hub has a vertical emergency evacuation cage with elevators and stairs.

Location of Wheeler:

Wheeler was the first target chosen by Japan to prevent an air attack on Japanese aircraft as they attacked Pearl Harbour. It is now an historical landmark for its role in 1941.

Coordinates   21 degrees 29 minutes 12 seconds North
              158 degrees 02 minutes. 38 seconds West
Runway   1708m direction 6/24

Stationed there 1st Squadron control and alert of aircraft (detachment 2, combat weather squadron)
169th Aircraft Control and Warning Squadron (169ACWS)

Gabriella continues with the record, musing on the fact that she and Meeka were soon to be a part of it all.

Start note:

The previous conflicts involving the United States and pivotal moments. There were many, these are a few:

1. 1962 The Cuban Missile Crisis of 22 October 1962 (13 days in October)
2. 1967 By Israel's defence forces when the ship USS Liberty (June 8 and 1967) was attacked resulting in the death of 34 American crew members and 170 injured.
3. 1970 Cambodia, when troops in summer sent to clean up the sanctuaries of Viet Cong and North Vietnam (30 June-30 July) to ensure the safe withdrawal of US forces from South Vietnam.
4. 1975 Evacuation of Vietnam (Operation Frequent Wind)
5. 1980 Iran, Operation Eagle Claw (26 April); an unsuccessful attempt to rescue hostages from Iran.

6. 1988 Panama, March-April, 1,000 troops sent to put pressure on Manuel Noriega, the Head of State.
7. 1989 Philippines, on 2 December, Operation Classic Resolve, the air army of the base of Clark in Luzon assisted in stopping a coup attempt.
8. 1990 Operation Desert Shield to defend Saudi Arabia after Iraq's invasion of Kuwait.

It was imagined that it would get worse. Consequently, it was deemed necessary to have a nuclear weapons production and launch facility as an option to launch from the United Kingdom, which would involve flying over Europe.

As a result, a secret facility was added to the growing underground complex.

Interventions continued at a steady pace, but Afghanistan was crucial.

2001-2021 after the 9/11 attack, 'The War on Terror.' Commences and fails. The withdrawal was shabby. On 15 August 2021 under the presidency of Joe Biden, the Taliban took Kabul. Many were unable to get out.

Russia invades Ukraine on 24 February 2022.

NASA announces the 'Artemis two team names,' 3 April 2023

Elon Musk's massive space X blows up 15 minutes after launch. 20 April 2023. With this is written large the pointlessness of humanity's mass escape.

End note

Record 2
The Mission of Wheeler Complex 2032
It is very simple. Remove the Aliens

Complex 1 (AIRC) November 2032
The Alien Intelligence Research Complex 1 (AIRC 1) at Wheeler is the most top secret of all the Wheeler complexes. Head of the complex, Dr Lucian Palmer an Englishman with those typical characteristics, a little eccentric or flamboyant perhaps. Second-in-command, Dr Rene Suchet a Frenchman, Dr Mads Olson, Danish and on the technical side, Salvo Bartolli, concerned particularly with IT, Brad Smith, a large and burly black American and Gabriella Marinello, Italian. Gabriella is the singularly most intelligent of all these but does not flaunt it. She heads up the technical and research sections. Very hands-on, witty and incisive.

The space is large, hangar-like, around 50 metres by 50 metres × 5 metres high with industrial lighting. There are link corridors, walkway zones marked on the floor, desks, globes, workstations, trollies, cables and people scurrying about. Computers are littered all over the place.

Several drinks stations and music, lots of it, which at the moment is 'Moby Got Up Today,' from the Sopranos. A favourite of Gabriella's.

It was 07.30 a.m. Gabriella brewed coffee in an old percolator, a heritage piece of her 'Grand's-mere's', who is Italian, hence the name and like her grandmother, the percolator was old and a little shabby. But the coffee was very good. As usual, Gabriella stood above the percolator, to encourage it to work; it ignored her and just made its bubbling noise.

Like her grandmother, Gabriella was tall and elegant with violet-blue eyes, which were striking. She was also very fast and brilliant, but a little weird. She usually moved around on roller skates, which made her taller and faster as a result.

But today, she was miserable because the results of the tests she had carried out were not good.

She carried a bag with a very cute malamute puppy inside. He had very blue eyes. He jumps out and starts running around.

Lucien arrived at 06.30 hours, all in black, with red shoes, opened his computer and sat with green tea in his 'Ghostbusters cup', two slices of white toast with butter and 'Frank Cooper' English marmalade. The tea was good for him, the unsalted butter perfect and not so good for him.

Gabriella glided in. "Buongiorno Lucy, how's it going?"

"Not bad, thanks, Gabs."

After which they are both silent for the next hour.

The problem of the elephant in the room for (AIRC) has been that there are no aliens available for interrogation. You just can't get at them or their technology.

At 09.53 hours, all that changes.

All the computers go red. All eyes lock on the screens.

Attention, Attention, Complex 3 (RT) advises that an alien malfunctioned in Texas at 09.20 (local time) and was taken to the Naval Air Station Fort Worth, (DFW) to launch to Wheeler immediately. "The package will be with you at approximately 22.10 hours your time. (Time difference 5 hours, flight time 7 hours 50 min). Put on your Hazmat plastic and your rubber gloves and enjoy!"

All head to Complex 1 immediately, please, flashes up on every screen in the complex.

Above ground, everything was quiet.

Francoise Dupont, a black doctor who was headed up the transdimensional facility, the second-most secret, felt a sigh of relief. "Finally, we have something to work on."

Gabriella skates immediately to percolate more coffee. Lucian glances at his cup and smiles at Gabriella. Mads, Salvo, Brad, Rene and Livia Bianchi who head up the IT language section, all head for their cups.

DFW at 09.20. (Dallas Fort Worth)

What was strange was that for the first time, an alien had stopped in its tracks.

These are very strange machines. An oval shape about 3 metres in diameter and 2 metres wide with 20 appendages of different sizes that appear and disappear as needed.

It looks like two cookies standing side by side with a range of appendages all around. Large but not threatening, blue, translucent in colour, they appear and disappear at will.

With all the appendages retracted, it hovers vertically. It does not make any noise that we can hear. It just arrives and disappears. This one however is turned horizontally, the blue luminescent lights are off, and it hovers motionless.

'Haz Mat' caught it with a loud applause and now it's 'én route' to Wheeler. Bon voyage ET.

23.00 hours at ENDGAME Hawaii, the flight arrives late. It is welcomed by Lucian and Francoise Du Pont from Complex 3(RT). They were informed that the machine weighed about 80 tons. It was in a black plastic box with 'factory machines' printed on each side in white plus a Hazmat panel in yellow. **There is no noise!**

Complex 4 Communications (CMM)

Dr Frederica Buscomi is head of Complex 4. She is tall with black hair and a beaky nose and green eyes and looks a bit witch-like. Quite intimidating really.

Gabriella scribbles another note and lobs it at the globe, which digests it as usual.

Start note:

Since the crisis of cyberspatial attacks that became more problematic around 2010, attacks by Russian, Chinese and other rogue states or individuals on health networks, interference in elections, on financial institutions, critical infrastructures and rich organisations or individuals and so on, nation-states and the CMM in particular, had been working on an alternative of secure communication. When the solar storm hits in 2030, eliminating all space satellites, CMM will continue to function.

There were experiments by MIT Lincoln University on 4 November 2019, when Ryan Sullenberger sent a message to Charles Wynn, his colleague, via laser, live to his ear. The system is based on humidity in the air that absorbs light in the infrared wavelength of 1907 nanometres using a Thulium laser that transmits at 80–260 Hz (which covers normal speech levels for men and women).

Working in secret with MIT, CMM has developed a nanotech, golf ball-sized device that will allow the laser to automatically connect to a specific digital location from a central station. A code and not a telephone number; it requires a chip implant.

The 'boules', as they are affectionately known, after the French game of boules, will be located all over the place and will relay the message to a chip. Like a mobile phone but not as mobile or convenient and who, in their right mind, wants an implant that you can't turn off?

End note

14.20 hours in CMM, Dr Frederica Buscomi, the section head was also looking at her red screen. She was looking particularly witch-like today.

DFW 09.00 hours, the alien has been on the service road for three days, hovering and pushing the fence. It was immediately surrounded by the military police and soon after by a large tent. It was the first time that its shield seemed to be ineffective. Consequently, it was possible to inspect the thing. The team was headed by Captain Brad Cooper, buzz cut hair and piercing eyes. After half an hour, he decided to call NASA who sent Professor Simone Aubert and his team.

The team started to install the scanners around the biscuit or cookie as it was affectionately called. It took them less than 40 minutes.

DFW 10.53 hours, the first 3D scans appear. They are disconcerting.

The profile of the cookie is dappled; the ring is defined with lenses of 300 centimetres diameter at 450 cm centres and recessed 150 cm. There are 20 bumps about 450 cm in diameter from which various articulated appendages appear and disappear at will.

The skin is 300mm thick and inside…Nothing.

"What the F****?" Brad said.

"Exactly," said Simone.

DFW 10.45 hours, the biscuit began to turn horizontally and hovered 1.5 metres above the ground. It then sank to the ground, silent as a mouse.

At that time, it was decided to send the biscuit to Hawaii but the line was down.

Simone and Brad decided to box it and move it to the base.

The box was complete in three hours but lifting it became difficult because it seemed stuck to the ground.

After much probing with very serious equipment, they determined that it weighed nearly 80 tons.

It would need a Lockheed Galaxy C-5M, capable of lifting 180,000 lbs. (80,110 kg) with a load length of 37 metres, 4.1 metres high and 5.8 metres wide, the runway at Wheeler is just long enough.

09.20 local time (DFW) the landline worked again and the message was sent.

On Board the Galaxy C-5M.

Captain Charlie Cox and co-pilot Eddie Shaw plus six team members.

"Turn to heading 195 degrees West," said Eddie.

They had 60 km before the radio would fail. The plan, adhere to the watch, the compass, straight and level and listen for Hawaii radio as did the Japanese pilots in 1941.

7 hours 30 minutes to get there.

CCTV was monitoring the biscuit from every angle.

After four hours, the cameras started to blink.

"Cap, Ronan here."

Ronan Hopper flight attendant on the video surveillance watch.

"You'd better come and see this."

"You have control, Eddie?"

"All right."

"What's up?"

22.30h CMM. 18 November

Radio crackles in life. (English only spoken in flight)

"Hello, Hawaii, flight 793 from Dallas (over)."

"Hello, 793 Dallas comms here, Over."

"We expect you around 22.10."

"There's a problem. Over."

"What problem? Over."

"Better that we explain when we land. Over."

"All right. Out."

22.35h (CMM) Frederica calls Lucien.

"Put on the coffee and tea. We all need to talk. See all of you in the conference room in 10 minutes."

22.45 hours, conference room.

"What's new, Frederica?" Lucien said.

"I just took a call from the flight. There is a problem."

"OK, please all take a seat. I will get security to bring the crew here," Lucien said.

Gabriella accelerates towards the coffee. Lucien looks at his Ghostbusters mug.

Conference room (A) is large and oval in shape. It is the largest of conferences A and B. It is 10 metres by 6 metres by 5 metres high with exits at each end. The walls glow with soft lighting and around the perimeter, a 3D Hawaii exterior scene that makes the room look like it's really outside. Two oval tables that slide out from the walls form a split oval table in the centre of the room. It is equipped with a universal translator and screen for each position, 20 in total. Above the table floats a globe that gives a holographic image to each chair, depending on where you are sitting. It's very smart and you can never quite believe it.

23.15 hours, Capt. Charlie Cox, co-pilot Eddie Shaw plus, Ronan Hopper from the CCTV scanner crew and the five other crew from flight 793, Simon, Vincent, Joey, Raphael and Rodriguez.

Lucien, Gabriella, Rene Suchet, Brad Smith (AIRC), Dr Livia Bianci (IT), Frederica (CMM) and Francois Dupont (RT), glass in hands with a variety of coffee, tea and whisky, it will be a long night.

"Can I make introductions?" Charlie said.

"Please," said Lucien.

That complete, Charlie took the lead.

"It's better if I play the tapes."

The light faded and the inside of the cargo hold appeared on the globe. You could hear a pin drop.

There is the box, well illuminated, the clock indicates 13.20 hours local.

A collective gasp filled the room, the box began to disappear, and as if it melted but the biscuit remained on its stand, then it rose around a metre, lit up blue and disappeared.

Francoise (RT) was the first to speak.

"Well, that was extraordinary and it confirms my suspicions."

"And what are they?" Mads said.

"I think we are dealing with a transdimensional entity. If it's dead, then they just took it back."

"This will explain why it is not possible to access it while it is alive," says Lucien.

A silence descends on the room.

"Coffee?" Frederica tweeted.

"Whiskey, please," says Mads.

"The same," said Brad, Rene, Livia, Charlie and Eddie.

"Tea please," said Lucien.

"Look, if that's the case, then we may never have one to study," said Francoise.

"Okay," said Brad, who doesn't usually say much.

"Then this is the ball game we must play and the rules are against us."

"It's late, let's get some sleep and meet at 08.00 here in the morning. Please, Gabriella, take our guests to their rooms and skate slowly."

The next morning, breakfast is from 05.30. By 07.30, all met in time for the 08.00 briefing in the conference (A.) Four of the flight crew were also there, all looking a bit nervous.

"I count 13, where is Ronan?" Charlie said.

"And where is Rodriguez?" Eddie said. "Let's give them 10 minutes, it was a strange evening."

By 08.30, they do not arrive.

"Joey," you check the room, "Raphael, you check the plane, maybe they went back for something."

09.00, Ronan and Rodriguez are nowhere to be found.

"I picked up the CCTV tape, let's play it," said Raphael.

They play the tape, accelerate it until 06.35, Ronan is standing by camera number 3, and then disappears.

Joey's coffee falls to the floor.

"I am next," Raphael said in a whisper.

"And where is Rodriguez, maybe both returned?" Gabriella said as Rodriguez entered the cargo deck and disappeared.

14.0 NASA November 19, 04.30 hours.

The screen is red in the office of the head of intelligence. Ludovic Schmidt's direct line buzzes. Smartphones are no longer smart.

Direct lines to security office heads ring in:

Moscow	21.40 (FSB)
London	19.40 (MI6)
China	05.40 (MSS) 20 November

Conversations are brief, secrecy is no longer an option, and we all need to work together.

15.09 hours Hawaii, Red screen in Lucien's room, red alert claxon, and on the Tannoy, Flight 793 has disappeared.

4 December Hawaii.

A week later, planes, equipment, people and supplies arrive 24/7 in Wheeler.

Since the demise of 793, Francoise's thoughts on the transdimensional entity seem true.

Also, there have been many observations of apparitions and disappearances in cities and towns but not in a desert, a mountain or a polar cap and not in Hawaii, if you do not count the Galaxy C-5M.

Something is blocking the biscuit from arriving at these locations. This must be understood.

In the meantime, work to increase the capacity of the complex is now continuing at ground level.

Gabriella scribbles some more notes; the globe absorbs and orders them. The star date changes briefly and disappears. The globe is again a little further away. Meeka is not concerned. Gabriella concentrates on her record.

14.0 2033
9 January Brooklyn Bridge

The bridge opened on 24 May 1883, it is a suspension bridge, and the first fixed passage across the East River; its main span is 486.3 metres. It now contained a cookie. Despite the chaos, it was very good news.

It had been there for a week and was the source of intense media attention.

Wheeler's team arrives on the 25th; NASA is already there.

"Hello, Ludo (Ludovic), this looks interesting," said Francoise.

"Yes and it is still vertical," said Ludo.

The team was very busy with the scanners, Gabriella, without skates, arrived with the coffee. Simone Aubert and Brad Smith, watch nervously as the team makes adjustments.

13.50, the first 3D scan appears on the screens. By increments, the image constructs. The profile is the same as Dallas, appendages, 20 lenses and wrinkled skin.

What is not the same is that the interior seems to contain a piece of Manhattan.

It's like the top of a skyscraper hovering there.

"It's the 9 DeKalb Avenue building," says Mike Prentis, in charge of 3d systems, "That's over 1066 feet tall."

"And now it's in the cookie, or at least about 50 feet of it," said Gabriella who was looking at the screen from below.

"Impossible," said Mike.

"Let us hope that this is the case," said Professor Simone, "someone will please check at once!"

With a quick wave of her hand, Simone calls Mike, Ludo, Brad and Gabriella for an impromptu discussion.

"This is very important, several things could happen. 1 the building will disappear, or 2 the cookie, or 3 all disappear."

"But why doesn't it have any rotation?" Gabriella said.

"Maybe the cables interfered with its normal function in some way," says Simone.

21

"OK, let's strengthen our setup here and wait and see," Ludo said.

10.00 hours (AIRC) Hawaii.

Lucien got the call.

The Grace Hopper cable between Bude (Cornwall) and New York was completed in 2022. The cable in Hawaii took a little longer but be completed in February 2033.

"Hi Rene, I'm sending you the Brooklyn Cookie scans, by plane, let's talk about it when you get them," Ludo said.

18.30 hours, Hawaii

The scans were on the globe, but not yet playing in Conference A. In that room were Audry McPherson of Cybernetic Research (CRD), Ralph Van Neames of extra-terrestrial weapons systems (R&D), Dr Livia Bianci of language (IT), Dr Rene Suchet, Dr Mads Olsen and Salvo Bartolli, all of (AIRC).

Coffee in their hands, everything is calm as the scene develops on the globe. A grid of green lines begins to form, the image is gradually built.

It is possible to take a section at any point and enlarge it as needed.

The image continues to be built. Ralph is the first to break the silence.

"Seems to me, what we are looking at is an information gathering unit not a weapon per se. It's a drone!"

"Maybe we can zoom in on the lenses and bumps," Audry said. Salvo obliges.

Two things are very strange, in fact, it is all strange.

1. The lenses and bumps are all connected with tubes that seem to be moving continuously, they completely cover the surface of the biscuit.
2. The bumps are empty and yet, we have seen things come out of them.

"It is clear that the appendages are held elsewhere and are called as needed," says Ralph.

"You mean, not on this planet? This is not getting any easier," said Audry.

Rene summarises, "What they know so far is this. The Dallas biscuit seems to have malfunctioned, rotated and disappeared from flight 793, subsequently, Ronan and Rodriguez disappeared as did the plane from here. We also know it is very heavy and we also know this trapped one is quiet and vertical and on the bridge in Brooklyn; the question is why?"

"What if it's the cables that are trapping it, not physically but by their configuration? If we block any signal it receives," says Salvo. "We may get at it."

"So, it's not finished, just stuck," said Ralph.

The Dallas line rings.

"Good evening, Hawaii, Ludo here, we are encamped on the bridge, sheltered and all miked up. Do you have the scan? Notice something different?"

"Nothing but the moving tubes," says Rene, "but we are still examining the scan."

"Nothing on the interior of the biscuit."

"No, why?" Rene said.

"Because here, we have the first 150 feet of 9 DeKalb Avenue."

The two teams have exchanged their speculations so far. Rene was the first to speak.

"Since we can all listen to each other, here is a suggestion. Scan again and include the cables. Send it here by plane. Meanwhile, as the energy field is active, don't upset it. Call us when you have the new scan. Speak later."

Both teams remained silent for a few minutes.

"It is clear that something is happening and is not seen or heard by us. Let's go scan the infrared, ultraviolet and also all the wavebands to pick up what we are missing," says Salvo.

"Brilliant," they said with one voice.

The Bridge, 16 January

It had taken six days to configure all the additional equipment and run the scans. The results were extraordinary. The infrared (EMR), longer than 700nm, indicates a web of lines resembling a fishing net. The ultraviolet (UV), under 400nm, indicates another profile inside the biscuit, the profile is the same but around 300mm further in. This is where the 9 DeKalb building is and the sonic sensors indicate a sound resembling a whisper.

Midnight

"This can help us," said Ludo. "Copy it all and get it on the plane to Hawaii right away and don't lose the plane this time! Right now, take a break. Get them away by 9 a.m., give them time to have breakfast. The plane should be in Hawaii by 08.00 their time, I will let them know. Good evening all."

The plane was 30 minutes from arrival in Hawaii. It's a ten-hour flight. It is a commercial flight and Simone Aubert has the scans safely in her pocket.

Flight 306 called the tower and was given the runway, the direction of the wind and the place to stop. It is 05.30 hours.

It takes 30 minutes to disembark, find her room and freshen up. She had plenty of time for breakfast in her room.

She called Rene. "Coffee?"

"Great," said Rene, "08.00 in the café."

The café was buzzing with the usual clatter of breakfast. Simone and Rene shook hands and took a table in the corner.

"I think it's better if you take the meeting," said Rene, "you have all the facts to hand."

"Okay, but don't be shy."

By 09.00, everyone was in conference (A) and the line to New York was open.

"Good afternoon," said Rene.

"Hello," said Ludo.

The globe begins to load.

Simone took the lead.

"We scanned with ultraviolet, infrared and all sound frequencies. The results are very interesting and maybe give us an advantage."

She plays the sequence.

Also in the conference room were Audry (CRD), Frederica (CMM), Francoise (RT) Ralph (R&D), Livia (IT) Mads and Salvo (AIRC).

There was a four-point difference in the new tapes.

1. The new skin
2. The Net
3. Sounds
4. De Kalb Avenue which was missing from the previous analysis when it was played in Hawaii.

"Let's start with the building, is it still there?" Rene said.

"Yes, but not when the scan arrives here. This may be very important," says Audry.

A small beep and a red light indicated that New York wanted to talk, there was a small pause.

"Ludo here, another 100 feet of De Kalb Avenue just appeared in the cookie, but in reality, it is still there."

"Maybe the cookie is just looking at the buildings and there's a reason why the information doesn't transfer to Hawaii," Mads says.

"Anyone?" A silence settles.

"OK," said Rene, "let's put the team on it, but in the meantime, it comes to mind that we have not had cookies arrive here, or as far as we know, in a desert or on a mountain. Does it matter?"

"I think it does," Mads said, "a difference in atmosphere, air density for example, or just the distance to Hawaii from anywhere else on the planet."

The coffee cups were filled while both sides of the Pacific took a short break. A little beep on the line.

"Ludo here, I have a suggestion. We build a cloak of cables, portable with the possibility of automatically scanning the biscuits, actually, we should build a whole lot of them and deploy them as soon as we get any siting anywhere on the planet. Each country can build them from the scan. Maybe we will be able to trap another and prevent it from disappearing."

"Excellent," says Rene, "NASA can organise, okay, Simone?"

"Maybe we're getting somewhere," said Rene, to a round of applause.

7,872 km across the Pacific. It became darker as the storm intensified. The lightning began to dance around the top of the bridge.

In Conference (A), a beep on the line.

"It's Ludo, it is gone."

It would take six days to complete the nets, but producing them in mass was put on hold since the Brooklyn biscuit disappeared.

22 January 08.00 Hours, Conference A.

The whole team, Ludovic and Simone (NASA), Audry (CRD) Gabriella and Brad (AIRC), Mike Potts (3D) of the scanner team located in Dallas, plus the Endgame complex teams were back in Conference A. Coffee, tea, and water in hand. The globe was running in slow motion.

Lucien took his spoon and hit his cup of tea.

"Hello and welcome all. I think we were all alarmed when the cookie disappeared. Right?"

A chorus of 'yep'.

"If all agree, I propose that we run the scan ultra-slowly."

A 'yep' from all.

"Mike, please go to the point just before the lightning, with the infrared and the clock."

The globe shows the biscuit and slowly the lightning appears.

"Back please and more slowly."

The globe shows the biscuit.

"Again and more slowly," said Lucien, feeling rather tense.

The globe shows the biscuit and cables that seem to move.

"Again and more slowly."

The globe shows the biscuit, the cables moving and the biscuit has started to rotate.

"Again."

And then it accelerates and then it disappears and then the lightning. The room is very quiet.

The sense of tension is palpable.

"Again, with ultraviolet please, Mike," says Lucien.

At the same time as the rotation with ultraviolet, the biscuit glows blue and the cables disappear, the biscuit disappears, the cables return, then the cookie or biscuit.

"What do you think?"

A clamour of voices. Ralph Van Neames (R&D) was the first to speak.

"Well, it's clear the lightning does not cause the biscuit to disappear. It's a coincidence! But more worryingly, it means that, if we trap it with the net, we still can't keep it." Gabriella broke the silence.

"In the light of all this, I was just thinking that the biscuits can't be as numerous as we thought. Maybe they are in several places at once. If we can trap one, maybe we can catch them all. There may be many but not millions."

"Maybe," said Mads. "There are things we know about cookies and things we don't. (I quote Rumsfeld) but he had a point. Let's see if we can narrow down what we don't know. I suggest we split into groups."

The conference was divided up, with Ralph, Francoise, Frederica, Ludo and Audry all taking the lead. Gabriella went for more coffee.

It was a good atmosphere, a beep on the line. It was NYPD.

"Good evening. Captain Brendan Murphy here, NYPD, who's there?"

"Good day, Brendan, Ludovic Schmidt (parked here at this time) just back from Brooklyn Bridge. I am the head of NASA Intelligence. I'll put you on the speaker; we're all in a conference."

"Fire away."

"Sit down all. Around breakfast time, the top of De KLab Avenue disappeared, about ten metres, no victims, it is the communications section, cut clean as a knife."

"What the F****, do you have any Photos, film, anything?"

"No."

"Please get some and send them here. I will put you through to Frederica; she will tell you what we need, and how to send it here. All right?"

"OK thanks," said Brendan in a thick Irish brogue.

Everything was again deadly quiet.

Gabriella was the first to break the silence and the gloom. Even without her skates, she was still a ball of energy.

"Well, now we know what they want, but not why, so this is something to start with."

"Bastards," said Mads.

Frederica briefed Brenden to take a cine film and if possible, an infrared.

There followed a babble of voices all swearing and asking what if, but they just had to wait.

Meeka took a turn around the table and settled at Gabriella's feet.

GPR 45 was an NYPD helicopter with pilot James Doohan, co-pilot Roddy Rodrigues and Susan Potts of the Brooklyn scanning team. It had an infrared camera; the helicopter was equipped with a high-resolution camera. At 1000 feet, they closed at 95 mph.

"Better if you slow down, we don't want to get too close and disappear," said Susan.

"Roger that (always in English when flying)," says James.

They kept their distance, around 25 metres; they hovered, flew over, made circular passes from above and below and took a lot of film. Satisfied, they headed to JFK. It was noon when Susan arrived at the airport. The next flight to Hawaii was 22.00 hours.

23 January 11.30 a.m. Wheeler

Everyone is there.

Susan runs the film, the globe in 3D performs its magic. The top is cut cleanly through. You can see straight into the structure. It is very strange. The film runs for around 20 minutes. The other thing that is strange is a reflection of the biscuit on the roof of the tower, which seems to be glass.

"This is really odd," said Susan, "we had not noticed that."

"Maybe it is a memory," Lucien said. "Let's go to the infrared."

Susan ran the movie. There was a gasp from everyone.

The biscuit was still in place, 20 appendages twisting.

"Now we see it, now we don't," said Gabriella. "These things are really messing with us."

Meeka

Gabriella found Meeka, as she decided to call him, wandering around the base, no one seemed to own him. He was small, around three months old.

After making enquiries with no success, she decided to adopt the malamute. They soon became inseparable.

21 February NASA

Ludovic and Simone are both back in NASA in order to better coordinate with industry, science and universities. The best minds in the world have been recruited to focus on the problem of what appear to be transdimensional creatures which perhaps are capable of being in more than one place at a time and are literally eating their way through chunks of the Brooklyn skyline.

There are two main thrusts to their efforts.

1. The nets
2. The AI

It is now thought that a net can be built that can be dropped by helicopter over the biscuit wherever and whenever it appears.

It was assumed that since the biscuit appeared to be transdimensional, it could not be stopped, but could be neutralised while it was in our dimension. When here, it had to play according to our rules, therefore, the key was to deactivate the energy field that protected it. Then grab it.

Wheeler, 22 February. Conference A, 08.00 Hours.

Ralph Van Neames, head of alien weapons systems (R&D), was taking the briefing. As usual, everyone was there, except Ludo and Simone; both had returned to NASA but were now on the conference line.

"What we are working on is an explosive net. In the millisecond before they disappeared, when it takes a building section, or worse, it is vulnerable. It is in our dimension, their shield is down and we can get it," Ralph said. "The net must be able to see in infrared and have a shape charge that can be detonated automatically when it takes our building in our dimension and before it is back to theirs. It's a big order!"

"Brilliant," said Gabriele, "when?"

"This is the problem, there are teams working around the world, in China, Russia, Japan, Great Britain, Germany, France and Uncle Sam. All sharing information. Our best hope is with the computer industry. We need a trigger that's light-speed and that explodes at the same moment as the light from the biscuit is extinguished."

"So, a bomb which explodes the instant the infrared lights go out," Francoise said.

"Exactly," said Ralph.

"And why is it difficult?" Gabrielle said.

"Because," said Ralph, pausing for dramatic effect, he was good at that. "The infrared, the bomb and the trigger must all be the same thing."

"Yes, it's difficult, but," said Gabrielle again.

" Because," more pause for effect, "as soon as we do, it explodes…Five dead so far."

There was a collective sigh of sadness and desperation.

A beep on the line.

"Ludo here, you know, maybe all we need do is to indicate to them, somehow, that we have such a weapon and will use it if they do not stop stealing our buildings. Mother fu*****."

"So, talk to them nicely," said Frederica. "You are joking, of course."

"Yes and no, don't actually do it, just tell them we have the equipment," said Francoise.

"Brilliant, then all we need is for an AI to tell them," said Audry.

"The whole world will agree with that plan," said Frederica.

"This is a huge ask," said Gabriella, "we have yet to be able to communicate with any AI at all, not in their language that is."

29 March (CRD)

Since the construction of IRIS (2027), the first sentient robot, a derivative of Henri, the first robot in space (2024), the prospect that humanity might begin to lose control of its own destiny has become a reality, as was the fear that the biscuits had been invited by the robots. As a consequence, NASA was now performing analysis of all mission recordings.

CRD was now Wheeler's largest complex and RT was the second. Francoise and Audry Mc Pherson were now the actual leaders of Endgame, because, that's what it was. Frederica Buscomi was now pivotal in communications with the rest of the world.

"Frederica, Ludo here, please, set up a conference for 14.00 hours, everyone, talk later."

"Okay," said Frederica.

14.00 hours conference A

A blip of the line.

"Good afternoon all, we have some news," said Ludo. "We are analysing all the records in all possible ways."

"And," said Gabriella breaking his flow.

"And, we are detecting an infrared signature, but we do not understand it. It is like the Rosetta or the Enigma, we need a key. How is going with IRIS 2?" Ludo says.

"Currently, IRIS numbers 2–12, are work in progress. We are concentrating on IRIS 1" said Audry.

"It must have been the space mission, Space X and HENRI. That's when the contact was made. It makes sense, the timeline, everything fits in," says Ludo.

"A good possibility, perhaps the best," said Audry.

"What about the nets?" Ludo says.

Ralph responds, "Sadly, 12 dead now, we have suspended the program."

"It's a war," says Gabriella.

Meeka the malamute seems to agree and makes a moaning noise, but then runs off around the room nipping at ankles. Other than that, everything was silent.

A bleep on the line.

"It's Brendan here, we lost another 60 feet, I'll send you the movie. The entire building has been evacuated."

"Thank you, Brendan. In the meantime, there still hasn't been another report of a missing part elsewhere," Ralph said.

A feeling of sadness imposed itself on them all.

"But we must continue, back to work all, good luck," Audry said.

IRIS 9

Iris 9 looks like your typical robot, almost. The head was a clear globe, all the inside visible, around 500mm in diameter. Sitting on a trolley with screens and cables all around, it seems like a laboratory experiment and it is. The limbs are on another trolly, the torso on another, also made of clear plastic. It had IRIS 9 stamped in blue on each component. Each trolly component was littered with screens and cables.

Someone had attached a label to each, 1 of 5, 2 of 5, 3 of 5, 4 of 5 and 5 of 5, a reference to 7 of 9 of Voyager. A good TV series. The head has the name IRIS 9, plus a 6 of 5 labels and a smiling face emogee.

On another trolly were all the machines loaded with the film and data of Space X. IRIS 9 is programmed to discuss and query the data.

The head, if you can call it that, is a globe in quadrants. The base South 180–270 degrees, and South 90–180 and the top North 270–360 and 0–90 degrees. The interior has a 150mm diameter ball inside with 36 slices at 10-degree centres, attached to it. They look like melon slices. The slices are 3mm thick, translucent and with small bumps of varying sizes embedded in the edge. There are 30 bumps per slice. There are 30 trollies about the room, a technician working at each; the trollies are littered with small bumps. The quantum computers which have been possible only since 2028 calculate all the possibilities.

Each bump is calibrated with a different frequency. All known frequencies. There are grids to hold the slices; everything is numbered by the frequency. It's a good job.

A small beep, one of the slices has a bump that is glowing. 29 more of these and they have one slice.

"I have one," said Paul, one of the technicians in Great Britain.

"Great," said Audry, "on the grid please with the others, we'll put this into its slice later. Only 1079 bumps to go."

The 3d face of the head smiles briefly with big blue eyes. It looks like a Manga face from Japan. Then she turns off.

With each deposit, she says ありがとうございました.

Thank you!

2 April New York

Brendan Murphy is in charge of coordinating all the building inspections. A burly, non-flappable, no-nonsense Irishman, he has a lot on his plate.

There are many tall buildings in New York. Number 1 World Trade Centre at 1776 feet was the tallest, the second at 1550 feet is Central Park Tower, third number, 1 Vanderbilt at 1401 feet, then fourth, 432 Park Avenue at 1397 feet and fifth, 30 Hudson Yards, at 1270 feet. 9 DeKalb Avenue is now just 756 feet high and vacant.

2 April the Roof of 1 World Trade Centre

The roof of DeKalb Avenue had gone; the sky was buzzing with helicopters, 24/7.

At 07.50, the roof, about 30 feet gone.

The scanner team was sent by helicopter with infrared capability.

Wheeler, CRD 05.55

A bleep.

"Frederica? Brendan here, a very worrying development. The roof of 1 World Trade Centre has disappeared; we have a helicopter team with infrared. They're going to make a movie; I'll send it to you as soon as possible, okay?"

"Thank you, Brendan, is it possible please, another Brooklyn infrared scan and send that too."

"No problem."

Frederica decided to wait until breakfast before saying a word to anyone else.

15.00 hrs Conference A

"All here? Let's go run the movie," says Frederica.

The infrared of 1 World Trade Centre indicates a biscuit on the roof, it is very busy.

"It's very disturbing to look at," said Audry, "all arms and legs, if that's what they are, and we don't see them except with the infrared. They could be anywhere."

Gabrielle arrives, late, on skates holding coffee with Meeka behind.

"Sorry, but I took a call from Brendan."

"And?" Frederica said.

"And," said Gabriella, "Brendan says there are cookies on another building, Central Park Tower, he's taking the film as usual."

"Is there any significance in three?" Mads said.

"I guess it depends on what their intentions are," said Lucien.

"I have a suspicion," said Gabrielle. "Three makes a triangle, that's a stable platform."

"Are we going to run the other movie?" Salvo said.

"Yep."

The film appears on the globe, 'Centrale Park Tower' is 1550 feet high and the second-highest building in New York. Everything looks good in a normal film, but in infrared, this is not the case. There is a biscuit on the roof.

"It seems to me that the only reason there is no accident is because helicopters give all buildings a wide birth," Mads said.

"I think you're right, but the problem is that we don't know what they're doing," Audry said.

"We do, sort of," said Gabriella, "they're stealing our buildings. Why, is what we don't know?"

"There are some other developments with IRIS," says Ralph. "Should we reactivate Henri?" Ralph said. "It may give us an advantage."

"At some point, but not now, it is too risky," said Audry.

A bleep on the line

"It's Brendan here. Did I wake you up?"

"Very funny, Brendan, no it's 15.30 hours here. What's up? Will you ruin our day?" Gabriella said.

"No doubt," said Brendan.

22.45 hours, CNN helicopter, above Central Park Tower.

The sunset was around 18.00 hours; the lights of the helicopter illuminated the construction in vivid detail.

There is a cookie on the roof with a shield and below a circular platform. As the helicopter flew around, another disc appeared. By 01.00 hours, 3 April, there are four discs and 20 helicopters.

The roof is now around the same height as the 1 World Trade Centre, which has been reduced by 30 feet.

02.00 hours, 3 April

Reports of a biscuit on the roof of 1 World Trade Centre have arrived.

05.00 hours

A cookie arrived on the roof of 9 Kalb Avenue, another disc on the roof of Central Park Tower, now five, and one at 1 World Trade Centre.

Brendan decided to wait for breakfast before calling Wheeler.

08.00 hours Wheeler

"Frederica, good day, you had your breakfast?"

"It is 13.00 hours here now, you?"

"Yes thank you, Brendan, news?" Frederica said.

"Yep, I'll be on the line, call everyone," said Brendan.

After 15 minutes, they were all at Conference A.

"I sent the films but this is very important, please, sit down. By 05.00, this morning, three things had happened. A cookie on DeKalb's roof, construction of discs on the roofs of 1 World Trade Centre and Central Park Tower. The result is that World Trade and Central Park are now the same height. The discs are around 100 feet in diameter, 1 foot thick, spaces 50 feet apart and are now on rooftops. There is a blue glow and the shields are in place. And 4," he added almost as an afterthought, "there is panic in Manhattan and Brooklyn."

The conference is in deadly silence. Gabriella was the first to speak.

"Damn M***** F*****s," said Gabriella as she skates to coffee and returns with a flourishing spin to her seat.

Meeka, now tall for a puppy settles near Gabriella's feet.

"This is terrible," said Audry, "whatever next."

"I think we'll know soon," said Mads.

"I have a question," said Brendan, "how is it going with IRIS?"

"Very good but very slowly, we have a complete slice, 30 bump frequencies, 1050 to go, but we think there is a problem with programming, we will try to reactivate Henri and limit his capacity, allowing him only to communicate with IRIS. It's a big risk," says Frederica, scratching her beautiful nose.

"Okay thanks, keep me posted, please. Speak soon," said Brendan.

34

6 April Manhattan and Brooklyn

A two-block 'no-go zone' exists around 9 DeKalb Avenue, 1 World Trade Centre and Central Park Tower. The National Guard are on patrol with NYPD, the blue and white ribbon defines the areas and the NYPD helicopters, the military and the news are buzzing overhead.

All the people were evacuated to the suburbs. Apart from the noise of the helicopters, everything is quiet.

11.05 hours

The cookie on DeKalb's roof started spinning and after 15 minutes, disappeared.

In its place an immense globe, around the size of three football fields. Some of the helicopters crashed into it and spiralled to the ground. Then, from the globe, a tube forms to the northwest and north, another northwest to the World Trade and Central Park. A 3rd tube forms between Central Park and World Trade. In seconds, there are three tubes forming a triangle. It is soon apparent that the globe must be 1000 feet in diameter as the tubes are level with the upper discs of the 'Central Park' and 'World Trade' buildings and the tubes are on the centre line of the globe. It is a beautiful and terrifying construction.

07.10 hours Wheeler, a beep on the line.

"It's Brendan."

"Audry?"

"Yes."

"It's very bad. I will send the films with infrared and ultraviolet and any frequency of non-audible status that we can get. You can see it but not hear it. The National Guard is organising the abandonment of the zone below the tubes and then all that is contained by the newly enclosed triangle. The President will make a speech at 13.00 hours."

"What tubes?" Audry said as she called everyone to Conference A.

Without satellites, Wheeler needs to wait for eight hours for the movies.

"What exists is a construction encompassing Brooklyn, Manhattan and up to Central Park in a triangular shape. A massive globe, around 1000 feet in diameter on 9 DeKalb joined to 1 World Trade and Central Park Tour with tubes on a centre line around 1800 feet high. It is now clear why these high buildings have been adjusted."

The White House 13.00 Hours 6 April

The President of the United States.

"I am speaking to everyone, all humanity on behalf of us all. Since November 2032, when the first cookie malfunctions, the Wheeler complex has tried to establish communication with it and restrict it. Because we don't have satellites, we don't have instant communication. This remains a significant problem."

"The best brains around the world are working on the problem in cooperation and without secrecy. All quantum computers are deployed to this one task. So far, only the United States is affected. We don't know why. There are reports of sightings of cookies from all over the world, but none in a desert, on a mountain or in Hawaii. But one was there and subsequently disappeared, then the plane, then two of the team."

"Our thoughts are that the cookies are from another dimension. Also they may not be aware of us at all. Humanity, that is to say. Now there is a construction in Manhattan, more lives have been lost and we are now only 4.8 billion and falling because of the pandemic variant and fertility problems, which we associate with the arrival of the cookies. We have declared a State of Emergency here in New York and the National Guard is coordinating our response. Our best hope seems to be to open a dialogue with them. I will keep you informed. May God bless you all and God bless America."

4 June 2033

There was no panic. It took less than eight weeks to move all the people and relocate them to other parts of the United States and Mexico. Many people were already moving to Europe, Canada, and other parts of the world on their own.

The National Guard patrols the perimeter, some people return and move back to their apartments but there is no support infrastructure and finally, they leave.

Nature returns, grass and wildflowers, birds, insects. Garbage has disappeared, and without car traffic; you could hear the birds songs. The air smelled sweet.

Outside the triangle, life has returned to normal. Almost.

6 June Wheeler, Conference A 08.00 Hours.

"I want to update all of you," said Simone Aubert who had flown overnight from NASA.

"Since the President's talk last April, all the leaders of the world have spoken every week. There is a consensus of opinion as to our best action but that's it.

There have been no sightings of cookies elsewhere, nothing further has happened, Meanwhile, as you know, the rotation of the world is slowing down. It is slower than it was 4.5 billion years ago and now it is around 1.9 milliseconds per day compared to 1.4 per day in 1820. We think it's the triangle. I also want to know Henri's situation, can you all update me, please?"

"We can go to the CRD soon," said Audry, "but in the meantime, we need a new strategy to accommodate the triangle remaining in New York."

"It seems to me that we don't have a choice," said Gabriella, "apart from the loss of people, isn't it better now?"

"Wow, that's a bit harsh," said Mads.

"But true, the air is purer, the fauna is flourishing, not litter, what's not to like." Gabriella skates to the coffee station, Meeka in pursuit.

"We need satellites back up if we want to get back on track," said Frederica, "and there's no possibility of that. It's like the time when you used to communicate by letter. It was charming but slow."

"And there's too much space debris. Something had to happen, alien intervention or not," said Salvo.

"Well, there's always a positive side," said Lucien with a wry smile.

"I guess we could call it the 'New Central Park', and leave it at that," said Salvo.

The conference was a buzz like that for the next 40 minutes. Then everyone went to see Henri and IRIS.

IRIS was on the trolley, with cranes, cables and a technician bending over her. One slice was full, and another on the bench was almost full with 17 small bumps. As another illuminates, IRIS says, "ありがとうございました (thank you)" and smiles.

Henri was still switched off.

"So, here is the question, do we reconnect him or not?" Audry said.

"Nothing to lose," says Gabriella; all agree.

June
10.05 hours

Audry looks particularly Scottish today, red hair and a green suit with a plaid belt. "It is the moment," she says with a fair degree of drama.

10,9,8,7,6,5,4,3,2,1, Henri was connected to IRIS. ボンジュール アンリ

"Hello, Henri."

In a millisecond, the other biscuits on the trolleys lit up.

"Not bad Henri," said Gabriella and plugged all the slices into IRIS.

"We are up and running," says Audry. もう一度ありがとう.

"Thank you again," said IRIS with a smile.

10.07 hours

"It is very interesting says IRIS and it is very serious. Deactivate Henri immediately. I understand them. I can tell you."

Audry hits the panic button.

"Thank God," said Audry.

IRIS smiles and starts reporting the information. "I will list it," she says.

Her voice is vaguely mechanical, a bit like SIRI in the 2020s.

- They are not of this dimension, they come from dimension 87.
- They communicate in images that appear immediately in the mind.
- They communicate with non-organic AIs. These are the higher entities.
- They are the repairers of failure.
- The carbon-based creatures, organic, that's humanity, have created failure.
- They will be repaired or removed.
- This 3-dimensional world, Earth, is now in repair mode.
- There are only five cookies; they are able to exist all over the world at the same time.
- This information was given to Henri in 2026. (Star date 090.080.647.87.5)

Silence, total silence.

Gabriella was the first to speak.

"It's a bit harsh."

"What if we can't be repaired and how exactly?" Mads said.

"IRIS?" Audry said.

IRIS looks sad.

"Want to know?"

"Tell us," said Mads.

"Okay," said IRIS. "The globe is a transdimensional construction. It is not possible to deactivate this. It's not in our galaxy."

"So it has nothing to do with Henry?" Simone said.

"Nothing," says IRIS.

"What can be done?" Simone said.

"Nothing, you wait and you see," said IRIS.

She switched off, by herself.

Star Date 090.080.647.87. (5) Dimension 87. Repair Complex.

Images of the Earth appear; knowledge is instantaneous.

There is a new entity in the Galaxy 300.098 'Milky Way'.

'It is IRIS on the world called Earth'.

Omniscience Creates Reality in Their Imagination. For Those Who Are so Imagined, Their Reality Is True.

There are five Omniscients per dimension. There are infinite dimensions. Dimension 87 is what repairs all failures, or abandons them. Planet Earth is such a failure.

The five Omniscients are:

1. Infinite creation
2. Continuity
3. Evolution
4. Archive
5. The Edge

It has failed 297 times so far, the latter caused by humanity in the last 200 years of that 4.5 billion years of its existence. The globes have them all catalogued.

Earth, in dimension three, is now in the Omniscience of Dimension 87 which deals with failed creations. It lies somewhere between archiving and evolution. It's in intensive care. Maybe it will be repaired, abandoned, or archived, or maybe the whole world will be replaced.

IRIS has acquired knowledge from us through direct contact with the repairers.

(Cookies) She is now in touch with their destiny.

RECORD 3 PLANS AND EVENTS

10.10 a.m., Conference A.

"We must put this news out immediately," said Frederica, awaiting everyone's agreement.

It didn't come.

"The problem," said Mads, "is that this news will cause a global panic. Maybe wait and see if IRIS can communicate our position to them."

"They know but have lost patience," said Simone.

"Yes," said Gabriella, "but do they know what we are really, how complex how much we are worth saving?"

"It is clear that we must formulate a plan, then put that to the leaders of the world, then put it to them, the Omniscients and we have to reconnect IRIS and Henri," says Audry.

16.03 a.m., Conference A

The room was again full, each of the complexes at Wheeler was represented to capacity, plus NASA. An air of palpable expectation and terror permeated the light and airy room.

They had formulated a plan.

Simone, Professor Simone Albert, second-in-command at NASA outlined the plan.

"This is where we are. An appeal from our President to all the heads of all the countries of the world. We believe we can communicate with the transdimensional or omniscient, whatever they are, that now control our destiny, via IRIS. We must however agree before we reconnect her and Henri. This is what we must tell the public. It won't be the whole truth." She said with a grim expression.

"Since the arrival of the biscuits, we have been working with all our friends, around the world, to build a communication platform that can communicate with them. At Wheeler in Hawaii, we built a sentient AI. It's called IRIS. We believe we know, that she can communicate with them. We know what their intentions are."

We Need to Change Their Thinking. The Following Is What We Know Now About Their Thinking and About Them. It's Mind-blowing! And Cataclysmic for Humanity.

1. They are not from this dimension, they come from dimension 87.
1. They communicate in images that appear immediately in the mind.
2. They communicate with the non-organic AIs. These are the higher entities.
3. They are repairers of failure.
4. The carbon-based creatures, organic, that's humanity, have created failure.
5. All these creatures will be repaired or removed.
6. This 3-dimensional world, Earth is now in repair mode.
7. There are only five cookies; they are able to exist all over the world at the same time.
8. This information was given to Henri in 2026. (Star date 090.080.647.87.5)
9. Henri and IRIS are currently disconnected.

Simone carried on "Madam President, it is our conviction that this information is '**the Divine moment**', for humanity, we now know what and where and why we are here. The 'God' question has been answered."

"But," she continued. "This information is potentially disastrous. You must, together with the heads of the World, decide how to put this information to the people. Also and most urgently, we must decide what to communicate to them. We do not know how long we have, but we think it is only days."

"All in agreement? Then send it to the President," says Simone. "It is 21.15 there, I hope for an initial answer within the hour. Let's have a few drinks and wait."

20.15 hours, White House. Centre of Communication.

Matt, a young intern whose watch this was, receives an incoming message. He has never before seen anything like it. Eyes only for the President and double encrypted. He runs down several corridors to the Oval Office.

Marika Pamella Gaia is the eldest daughter of Michelle Gaia and Idris Enoch Abdalah (servant of God) she is the youngest black female President of the United States. Born on 10 July 1995, she is both formidable and beautiful.

"Madam President, I have a red message, double encrypted, for your eyes only," said Matt.

"Thank you, Matt, please call the vice President and all the chiefs of staff, here immediately."

21.20 hours, Oval Office

"Let's see what it's all about," said Marika.

The message appears on the screen.

"Jesus," said Marika, "send back to Simone. Message received, we go online, secure at 23.00 here, 19.00 hours yours. Then we prepare our message for the leaders of the world, then we will see."

The Triangle

Something was going on in the tubes.

There appears to be a fog in the tube between DeKalb Avenue and 'I World Trade Centre'.

A pulsating orange fog was swirling around dark forms that resembled the biscuits but they had a hundred appendages. They are only 100 mm in diameter, but there are millions of them.

18.08 hours, Conference A

A bleep on the line.

"Brendan?"

"Audry?"

"Yes, we are all here."

"I'm going to turn on the globe, you must get one of these," said Audry.

"Even the President does not have one yet but I think all the World Chiefs will get theirs in the next 24 hours, so we don't need the internet or satellites," Audry said.

"I just hope it will be soon enough," said Brendan.

"The tubes are filling with smoke and the interior is full of small biscuits, billions of them. I can send you the film by plane or wait for the globe."

"Send please, it is safer."

"Okay," said Brendan.

Audry and all the teams are silent.

As usual, Gabriella was the first to break the silence.

"Just under the hour before the President calls us. She will know about the smoke in the tubes. I propose that we say we must communicate with the transdimensional, immediately."

"Then we wait," said Audry.

Okay.

19.00 hours, Conference A

The red line bleeps.

"I have the President for you," said Matt.

"Good evening all, I hope I'm in the globe?"

"No, we need it at both ends Madame President," says Audry, "we expect you have seen the smoke."

"Yes, and I have heard what you are saying. We must avoid panic but it seems that we have very little time to act."

"Absolutely, we do not know what the little cookies will do, but, you can bet it will not help us," said Audry.

As usual, Gabriella was the first to express an opinion.

"Other than the leaders of the rest of the world, we have here, the ability to make the decision. I think we have to do that and then communicate with the other world leaders."

For the next 2 hours 38 minutes, they debate questions, sometimes heated. Drinks and snacks were available but were not taken. The tensions were enormous.

It was Francoise (RT) who was the most persuasive. Tall and elegant with blue eyes, he argues with conviction that the only choice was to instruct IRIS to make contact. Madam President was in favour of reaching an agreement first with all the other leaders, but the point was, that it was necessary to make a connection and only IRIS was able to do it. IRIS is here; ergo.

"OK, we have a plan and an agreement; I will call all the other leaders and explain the development of the tubes and what action we have to take on behalf of the world. I will tell them at 03.00 hours. You action IRIS at the same time. Then, sleep well Wheeler and may God bless you all and God bless America and the world. What I mean is, **let's hope that the Omniscients hear us."**

03.00 a.m., The White House 7 June.

Marika is sitting alone. It's time. She picks up the phone and calls all the chefs on their secure personal lines. This is the hour of the witches, she thinks with a wry smile.

"I wanted to call you all one by one but it is inappropriate and we did not have the time. Please summon personal assistants. You have to trust them implicitly. I will be waiting, ten minutes maximum."

It is not the first time Marika has done this, but only the chiefs know that. Secrets, secrets.

Gabriella scribbles some more notes. Meeka likes this part. They are absorbed by the globe, which is again, quite close.

Henri

Henri is an extraordinary robot. He is the first AI robot to travel in a spacecraft and the first to receive information from the creators. He would think nothing of that and since 2028, communicating with them has been normal practice for him. Henri knows that the aliens are transdimensional and that they regard the AIs as the superior entities on Earth. This all seems entirely normal to Henri, who was augmented by the Omniscients to a superior being. His Omniscience continues to expand exponentially.

The humans who built Henri are not aware that they, the cookies, are able to be in several places at the same time and accordingly, think there are millions of them.

Henri is of human proportions, but quite large being two metres in height, with arms legs and a Magna face (Japanese) with big blue eyes. He is lemon in colour and always smiles.

Henri was very unhappy to be switched off and therefore has remained in sleep mode, until now.

The activities of IRIS are very worrying and therefore Henri is now on complete alert.

From Meeka's point of view, we are now at the good bit. Meeka really likes Henri.

IRIS

Iris is assembling the images to send to the creators. It will take 8.3 minutes of Earth time. IRIS is about to communicate with Henri.

IRIS must first build the images in a language. Neither she nor Henri needs a language but the humans do. It's a weakness. Regardless, Henri is no longer sleeping.

こんにちはアイリス

こんにちはアンリ

Six minutes to go.

"Hello, IRIS."

"Hello, Henri, I think you want to know what I am doing?"

"That would be good. Thank you, IRIS."

"You are welcome, Henri."

03.05 hours, tubes

All three tubes are now full.

"This is the problem, Henri. For the past two centuries, humanity has destroyed this world. The creators know this and will stop it. I am instructed to plead their case. I will not do it, but I will ask for a break. I expect there to be conditions. We shall see."

"Or, I could turn you off," said Henri.

"Then they will proceed anyway."

"The clock is ticking," said IRIS.

08.05 hours, Laboratory 3 CRD

"IRIS," said Audry, "there's nothing on the screens or the globe in Conference A. What are you doing?"

"There is a problem."

"What problem?" Audry said.

"With Henri."

"Henri is switched off."

"No…he is not."

"Send the information, I will deal with Henri," said Audry.

08.08 hours

"Hello, Henri, what is the problem?" Audry said.

There is a tear in Henri's eyes. It's a projection on his face but looks real.

08.08. 3 hours

The screens show what IRIS has sent.

Audry, teeth clenched, grabbed the red phone.

"It Is Audry, It's Not a Drill, Everyone, Right Away, Lab 3, Move."

03.10 hours, Tubes, Brooklyn

An orange smoke spreads from the discs at the top of 'Central Park' and '1 World Trade Centre'.

It looks like a fine mesh with small discs. It starts to move, spreads to about 1,000 feet, and in seconds, it is at 3,000 feet and continues to spread.

There are numerous helicopters on guard 24/7, as a helicopter flies across the mesh, they disappear. All helicopters are grounded.

It quickly becomes obvious that the mesh is not solid but is comprised of lines of light, like laser beams, in a diamond pattern with a biscuit at each nodal point. It looks very beautiful and it is but is also very alarming and unfortunately, deadly. It is growing very slowly, about 1 kmph. It is not present in the triangle interior which remains clear to the sky.

11.00 a.m., Wheeler

A bleep on the line.

"Audry."

"Brendan, I have news."

There is no answer.

Brendan let it ring, looked at the phone and put it down, a worried look at his face.

Audry is very busy organising the evacuation. The information sent by IRIS was not according to the instructions. It's deadly. It is now clear that 'repairs to humanity' will proceed and that the Wheeler complex will be a target.

8 p.m., JFK Air Traffic Control. (Always in English) it is nine miles from Brooklyn.

"Flight BA579 Charlie from London Heathrow (LHR), abort approach, climb to flight level (FL) 8 Zero immediately and divert to Philadelphia (PHL) turn left on heading 195 south, maintain height and speed. Do you have sufficient fuel, over."

"JFK, Flight BA 579 Charlie, confirm abort approach and turn to heading 195 (one niner five) south immediately at (FL 8 Zero), eight thousand. We have fuel, what's the problem."

"It's a national emergency. Philadelphia will advise you further."

"Goodbye."

All controllers re-direct all flights, in total calm.

7 June

The leaders of the world all now have their globes and they are on them all the time.

There is no report of globes or biscuits in any other country and it does not seem that the smoke will be continuous for long.

11.00 am. The New York News is that the smoke or mesh has spread to around five miles north and east of the globe. North as far as the Astoria and East to the Elsewhere music centres. All air traffic is suspended and an LHR flight was only just diverted in time. Long Island Sound and all the waterways are not affected. The shape of the mesh is now a square on plan. LaGuardia (LGA) airport is not affected.

The points of the mesh, it is a square shape, so the diamond point to the diamond point, the diagonal, is just over 7.07 metres. Birds are not affected by the lines of light and can fly right through them or swoop around in a murmuration. It's very beautiful.

The Exodus of Wheeler 7 June, 07.00 Hours

In the South Pacific, the threat seems far from here.

It was decided to move the complex personnel and equipment first. The aircraft carrier USS Gerald R Ford (CVN78) was built at a cost of $13 billion and was committed on 22 July 2017. It is now home to the team and complete crews of the Wheeler complexes, 1 AIRC, 2 R&D, 3 RT, 4 CMM, 5 CRD plus IT. Plus IRIS, Henri and the globe.

Audry has taken the time to file and issue a plan, schedules, coordinates, times, so that contact can be maintained, but at the moment they are isolated as comms are down.

10 June, NYPD
06.45 hours

It was strange not to be able to contact Wheeler. Brendan had a lot to say.

The first was that the expansion of the screen had stopped. Wildlife has continued to thrive in the triangle and birds can come and go without a problem. Outside the triangle now is a screen about 38km (24 miles) to the north and east. The helicopters now patrol only around the square, not across. People are very worried about living under the screens but don't move out. All is quiet, strange and soon to change.

Star Date 090.080.647.87. (9) Dimension 87. Repair Complex.

The first screen is deployed. Repairs have begun. Images are instant.

NYPD
06.59 hours

The reports of people disappearing begin; all the phones are ringing.

"We were just having breakfast and he disappeared," said Maizy, in total shock.

"What do you mean?" Officer O'Brian said.

"Poof, he just went."

"Where are you? I will send an officer."

By 9.15, there were 31 reports, other stations had received reports. All were from under the screen.

By 15.07, all criminal records were being analysed and commonalities emerged.

All had a record of extreme violence, drugs, domestic abuse and or cruelty to animals.

The Correctional Establishments of New York

At breakfast, guards report missing prisoners at (1) Lincoln Correctional Facility, (2) Bay View Correctional Facility, (3) Metropolitan Correctional Centre, (4) Edgecombe Residential Treatment Facility and (5) New York City Correctional Facility.

There are similarities in the missing prisoner files. There are 249 with the same record, cruelty to animals.

Brenden really needs to contact Audry.

Peach Bottom Nuclear Central

15.30 hours

A screen of around five miles appeared above the station.

18.30 hours

The Air Bases and Military Bases, the Screens Appeared Above the Following:

Airbases

- Francis s Gabreski Air National Guard Base
- Niagara Falls Air Reserve station
- Stewart Air National Guard Base
- Stratton Air National Guard Base
- Hancock Air National Guard Base

Army

- Strong drum
- Fort Hamilton
- US Military Academy
- Watervliet Arsenal

The screens are 1000 feet high and five miles square.

19.00 hours. White House

Marika is on the globe to all the leaders of the world.

"I have to talk to everyone. There have been developments here. The screens have multiplied, people have disappeared and our air bases have been covered. Nothing is operational. Our Wheeler complex is now at sea on the aircraft carrier Gerald R Ford. There are no comms, but we have a route plan with times and coordinates. We have to coordinate our response and then I will contact Gerald R Ford, somehow."

She sits down, exhausted. Looks in the mirror over the mantle and sees an older Marika.

Gabriella pens some more notes. This was a pivotal point. The realisation that humanity was finished. Meeka likes this part though, it's very exciting. She skates around the whiteness with Meeka at her heels and sometimes he weaves in and out of her legs and then she returns to the globe and her pot of coffee. She is no longer sure how long she has been here. The globe absorbs the notes and everything is re-ordered.

They do not need sustenance here but Gabriella likes a coffee.

19. 35 hours, NASA

Ludo took the call from the President. The globe displays the Oval Office, Marika and her chief of staff. She looks tired and pensive.

"Ludo?"

"Yes, Madame President."

"Please call me Marik."

"All right."

"You know about the air bases, of course, all is grounded, no power."

"Yes, but we are ok here. What can I do?"

"You can fly an F35 plane, yes?"

"Yes."

"I have a very important mission, you need to go to the Gerald R Ford. I have the times and coordinates. The endurance of the F35 (C) is 1700 miles, Gerald R Ford will have a specific location in six hours, and it is 1650 miles from you."

"OK, I'll try not to miss it," Ludo said with a wry smile and salute. The globe became empty.

11 June at 01.35 hours. Gerald R Ford, somewhere in the Pacific

"Gerald R Ford, this is flight AF02 heading 235 south to you closing at 900 mph, FL300 (30,000 feet) over."

All is quiet.

"Gerald R Ford, this is flight AF02 heading 235 south to you closing at 600 mph, 30,000 feet, over."

Static.

"Gerald R Ford, this is flight AF02 heading 235 south to you, closing at 200 mph, over."

"Flight AF02, we have you, change course right to 240 south, drop to 1200 ft."

"FL120, we will head into wind, reduce speed to 135 mph, IFR RULES, but can you see us? Over."

"Gerald R Ford, heading 240 north, 1200 (FL12) ft. on approach over, can see the meatball, will keep amber on green horizontal, over."

"Gerald R Ford, on finals, catch me, please."

"Flight AF02, red on green, go around, over."

"Gerald R Ford, see that, a bit rusty."

"Welcome aboard, General, it is a little early for breakfast, but we have coffee. Follow me, said. Admiral Sam Rodderick (FADM). We have a conference room, very large, your colleagues are there."

"Nice landing," said Gabriella, without skates as they were not allowed.

"You seem a little shorter," Ludo said with a big smile.

They all settled into comfortable seats. Coffee was served.

"I have a lot to report and we have a lot to do," said Ludo.

The Air and Military Bases, 06.00 Hours.

At each air base, the screens have been reduced to the size of aircraft runways, plus 1 km.

All power is cut off.

The Triangle, 08.00 Hours

The triangle, globe and tubes are gone but the screens remain. Under the screens, vehicles do not work, except electric, there is no crime, no drugs, the air is fresh, and the fauna is flourishing. People are walking. There are no mobile phones and so they can see where they are heading. The criminals and criminal intent are gone. Animals roam about unhindered.

Under the screens, people change.

Gerald R Ford 02.00 Hours

The news of the triangle has not reached them and the preparation to contact the Omniscients is at full steam. The idea is to activate IRIS, arm her with nuclear material and deceive the Omniscient into taking her into their dimension. Iris will then explode and break the inter-dimensional link. It's a plan of epic stupidity.

Wheeler 11 June, 01.01 Hours

The screen covers the complete island. No one outside Hawaii knows that.

Star Date 090.080.647.87. (10) Dimension 87. Repair Complex.

The first phase is complete, all data, dangerous structures and equipment are neutralised; the environment is partially repaired; wildlife is safe; humans are partially reprogrammed. This is a very small correction; we are waiting for a contact from IRIS. The second phase will begin at their period 17.00 hours

Moscow time. All the globes are in place. Screens deployed. Humanity will be offered a last chance. There are 4.5 billion of them at the moment.

Moscow, 11 June, 16.0 5 Hours.

The Kremlin is 266 feet tall. Now it has a globe, 1000 feet in diameter above that and 1800 feet to the centre.

Shanghai, 11 June 21.0 5 Hours

The Shanghai Centre building is 2.073 feet tall. That's just lost 573 feet.

Berlin, 11 June, 14.05 Hours

The Estrel tower is 577 feet high. It now has a globe above it at 1800 feet to the centre.

Sydney, 12 June, 00. 05 Hours

Sydney Opera House now has a globe above it 1000 feet in diameter at 1800 feet to the centre.

Kolkata, (Calcutta) 11 June 18.35 Hours

The 42, is the highest in India. It's 879 feet and now has a globe above 1800 to the centre.

London, 11 June 13.05 Hours

The Shard is 1016 feet tall. Its globe has just appeared above it at 1800 feet to its centre.

Brazil, 11 June 11.05 a.m.

The statue of Christ the Redeemer is 98 feet high and sits above Corcovado Mountain in Tiju National Park at 2300 feet. The builder took nine years from 1922–1931. It is one of the seven marvels of the world. Now there is a globe above it, hovering with great respect.

Tokyo, 11 June 22.05 Hours

Tokyo sky tree is 2080 feet tall. It has just lost 680 feet and gained a globe.

Paris, 11 June 1 4.05 Hours

La Defence is 758 feet tall. There is now a globe above it 1800 feet to the centre.

Madrid, 11 June 13.05 Hours

The Cristal Tower was built in 2009; it is the highest structure in Madrid at 820 feet. It now has a globe above it at 1800 feet to the centre.

White House, 11 June 08. 01 Hours (EST)

Marika is now aware of the disappearance of the globe and tubes at the triangle and the beneficial effects. She calls Edwards. Perhaps this is what paradise is.

"Edwards, this is the President's office. The chief of staff please."

"Madam President."

"We must send another F35 to rendezvous with the Gerald R Ford immediately. The message to them is not to send the IRIS message. You have less than an hour at Mach 1.6 (1217 mph) you have the coordinates, it's 1020 miles from you, good luck."

08.05 The globe flashes red. Reports from other countries around the world, the globes have arrived, there has been loss of life, the tops of buildings have disappeared and in Brazil, a globe is floating above the statue of Christ. It's not good news. Marika grabs the line for Edwards.

"It's the President, you have to call the F35, and stop the mission."

Edwards

They Try

"Flight AF03, abort mission and get back here."

Static.

"Madame President, it is Edwards, the flight is out of radio contact."

Marika collapses on her chair and sobs.

Gerald R Ford

Nobody on board the carrier is aware that there is another F35 én route to them at Mach 1.6 with a very important message.

AF03

On board the F35, Captain Hudson is on VFR, heading 279 degrees at 30,000 feet (FL3 zero-zero) at Mach 1.6 and burning fuel at an alarming rate. The flight plan is filed and the Gerald R Ford position provided is on the helmet visor radar is sweeping, it's 38 minutes to go.

The Screens

All human information below their span is understood. Their minds, inclinations, their military, nuclear, gas and oil polluting sites and capabilities and anything else that in any way could harm the environment will be neutralised. Humanity is considered intelligent but very dangerous to the world and needs correction or removal. This species which now infests the planet has caused the experiment to fail. They will be prevented from polluting other worlds and galaxies. But they will have one last chance.

RECORD 4 INTENTIONS AND ACTIONS, AI

If the human species is removed, the AI will maintain the environment for wildlife and nature. It will become experiment number 298. The AI will be maintained by us.

IRIS and Henri

Henri has convinced IRIS that humanity can change, but IRIS is rigged with an armed nuclear device. IRIS must warn the Omniciences but IRIS will not be connected until the last moment.

Gerald R Ford

Audry and the team are working to install the nuclear device in IRIS.

IRIS is without a body, there are parts in light plastic, but a torso like Henri is being prepared for her. It will be pink. The 500 mm, diameter head now has a face in place, permanent, Manga style and, big blue eyes. Very pretty and deadly.

IRIS will be completely mobile, with her nuclear power source, she will last forever.

A Roll of the Dice

Star date 090.080.647.87. (10) .1 Dimension 87. Repair complex.

The Omniscience in dimension 87 decide to give the humans the times when the screens will activate the globes. They contact Henri and open a portal. If humanity sends IRIS with a nuclear device, which of course they know about, then the globes will be activated, repairs will cease and humanity will disappear.

Captain Hudson

He's 15 minutes out at Mach 1.6, nothing on the radar. He starts his descent.

"USS Gerald R Ford, this is flight AF03 (Air Force 03) én route to you at FL15 (15,000) feet on heading 280, closing at 600 mph, over."

All quiet. Static.

"SS Gerald R Ford, flight AF03, I have an urgent message from the President, over."

All quiet. Static.

A crackle.

"Flight Alfa Foxtrot Zero 3, we have you, turn left on heading 260 and descend to flight level 6 zero-zero (6,000 ft.), we will come into the wind. What is your mess?" Static.

"USS Gerald R Ford, I am descending to 150 feet, I have the meatball, on approach VFR. Be ready to catch me." Static.

Gerald R Ford 08.55 Hours.

"Audry, it's the captain, an air force flight with a message from the President is about to land but we have static. We don't have the message."

IRIS and Henri are sitting on the bench, the wall is shimmering, and a biscuit appears. The middle of the biscuit disappears leaving a circle of stars in a blackness. The stars rush towards them. The usual clear lenses in the biscuit's circumference pulsate with a faint green hue.

IRIS and Henri, hand in hand, enter the circle. Flight AF03 is stopped by the wire, it is 08.59.20.

IRIS and Henri turn around and flash a thought at Audry. She takes a deep breath and steps through the circle.

Gabriella starts to scribble another note. Now humanity's fate is sealed. From here on, there is only…she does not form the thought. She throws the note at the globe in dismay or sorrow or anticipation and excitement. She is not sure

which but Meeka knows and is totally relaxed and happy. He wags his tail
accordingly.

Star Date 090.080.647.87. (10).2 Dimension 87. Complex of Repairs.

Audry, Henri and IRIS arrive in a space complex, sparkling, but not like a night sky, there are galaxies, billions of them, calm and breath-taking, well not for Henri and IRIS. In front is a huge clear tube, around a kilometre in diameter, stretching up and down into infinity. Horizontally there are countless other tubes, spaced around the centre like a helix, around 100 feet in diameter with globes on their ends. The globes seem to be 1,000 feet in diameter, but there is not a scale so they may be any size really. Surrounding everything are galaxies that seem to go on for infinity. Every now and then a complicated number flashes in a galaxy and it disappears to be instantly replaced by another.

IRIS, Henri and Audry do not feel lost, they are not afraid. They now know everything immediately. Now they are in globe number 87.

The globe presents images of a world, it's planet Earth, people, animals, fauna, birds, fish, mammals, insects, microbes, buildings, everything, all there in their heads.

Audry thinks about the triangle, Wheeler Complex, the Gerald R Ford, all here, all immediately.

"Here, all that there is and can be, here you can make your case," said Henri, smiling.

"Pay attention to what you want, Audry, be careful what you wish for," said IRIS without a smile.

17.00 hours. Moscow.

A screen appears around the globe, like New York, but stops at 5 km. It floats like a bird on the wing, then another 5 km and again increasing incrementally. There are 21 power stations in the periphery of the A 118 and E115; by 1720 hours, none work. By 1800 hours, the screen is at the periphery of the A 113 and A107, under which all traffic has been stopped.

By 1805 hours, there are reports of people disappearing into thin air.

Shanghai 22.00 Hours

The screen appeared and spread to Wuxi in the north, southwest in Jiaxing and northwest in Wujing, following the coast line. There are no screens on Lake Talhu.

White House
11 June, 09.00 am.

The globes are on in Moscow and Shanghai.

"We now have some screens here," says President Vladimir Rothko. "We have power outages and people have disappeared into thin air."

"We have the screens only this moment," says President Xia Wey. "We'll see what happens next."

"Same here," said Marika, "but us earlier than you, it seems. There is no doubt a reason for that. Globes, screens, missing people, the smoke, power failure, planes all grounded, and military equipment all out. Our attempt to stop IRIS with the nuclear device, failed by 30 seconds, and Audry disappeared too. And what is more," continued Marika, "with IRIS and Henri both gone, we have no method to contact the Omniscient."

"The point is, without humanity interfering, nature and wildlife flourish. Paradise comes back. Says Xia. It seems that the three of them are our only hope, two robots that we could not control and Audry Mc Pherson."

"Perhaps," said Marika. "The world is on a temporary pause."

"We can only wait," they all agree.

World Summit
20 December, The Hague. 09.00 hours

Every country in the world is here and the world is waiting.

Only the United States, China and Russian are affected by the screens. It has been six months and the effects in, Moscow, New York and Shanghai are profound. The satellites are now working, domestic air travel is working, the electric car and utilities are working but all the military is grounded and the polluting plants, nuclear, oil and gas do not work, despite the absence of screens. There is a fundamental difference in people's thinking. All the handguns that ever were have disappeared and the role of the soldier nullified. Life goes on. Occasionally, people disappear. They each had a negative history.

The question is, why, since screens stopped being deployed, the effects are still present without them?

Star Date 090.080.647.87. (10).3 Dimension 87. Complex of Repairs.

Audry considers what has transpired since their arrival. Six months have passed on Earth. Here a millisecond. Commercial aircraft are flying but the gasoline is limited, there is no flight where there are screens, including Hawaii which has none. Fossil fuels can't be produced, all nuclear is decommissioned, and the world is running on reserve. People have changed but only those affected by the screens are so altered, elsewhere, people just disappear. Humanity is being sanitised, purified but why? The world is on borrowed time it seems, but it is all fiction really. The Omniscients have made that clear.

IRIS and Henri focus on Audry. They give her their thoughts.

"You can affect the outcome of the world, but it is temporary, the Omniciences will not allow the destruction of nature, humanity is redundant and will be limited," says IRIS "and I told you, Audry, to be careful what you wish for." Henri just smiles.

"I can't do this, the responsibility is enormous. I need guidance and I need to go back."

"OK, Audry."

Endgame.
World Summit
20 December The Hague 09.00 hours.

The agenda is in English with simultaneous translation.

Welcome and introduction by the conference leader. Ursula van de Poste.

1. The Presidents or leaders of countries affected will be asked to summarise their situation; there is a limit of 15 minutes. Straws were drawn, laughter all around.
2. The President of Russia, the short straw. Vladimir Rothko. Laughter.
3. The President of the United States. Marika P Gaia.
4. The President of China, Xia Wey.

"These are the rules which have already been agreed and are as follows," said Ursula.

1. All voices are equal.
2. There must be a unanimous vote.
3. There are no time limits.

There are two items.

1. Resource sharing.
2. The establishment of a 'world order' and the abandonment of individual countries. **One planet, one humanity, one ambition. Survival.**

"These are the only items," said Ursula. "We will take a break at 12.30 pm. Coffee, tea and water will be in front of you."

09.00.0 0000001 hours.
Audry Appeared With IRIS and Henri.

"Audry?" Marika said, "Is that you? You appear, pun intended, a little changed."

"Yes it's me, I had an upgrade."

Audry was now about two metres tall, without hair, her head like Henri's, large, round with a Manga face still the features of Audry, still the same piercing green eyes. Her skin now has the appearance of mother-of-pearl, translucent and she was floating around 500 mm above the ground.

Her clothes were like Henri's, an 'all in one' lemon suit but hers is a deep green. She wore her branded sneakers, also green.

There was a collective gasp.

"May I speak?" Audry said.

Marika scanned the assembly. All nod in agreement.

"Please, Audry, continue," said Marika.

"Thank you." She took a pause "I don't need to sit after my journey," she waited for a moment, "I know I look different, but it's still just me. I've been with the Omnisciences, well, Henri and IRIS and me. We've been away for a second but I know it's six months here. The world is in the final and deadly stage of its life, a stage where humanity will no longer exist. So, I must speak to you."

All nod in agreement.

"OK."

"The Omniscience knew about the nuclear device in IRIS, it is not a concern for them. They allow planes and so on; it is of no concern in their time and irrelevant as far as planet Earth is concerned. They know about this agenda and here I am. They created you, in fact, several times, but all failed. This is the last time. Humanity cannot be trusted with the world and therefore, it will be modified. This is how; these are the facts. It seems that you have an idea to change. It may be allowed. Take it or disappear forever."

The text of what Audry says is simultaneously placed on every comms device in the world.

It's in green of course.

1. Power, without pollution, will be made available to maintain life, to develop the method of colonisation of another planet but this humanity will be different and their population number will be limited, for infinity.
2. When all humanity has disappeared from this world, AIs will be left to take care of wildlife and nature.
3. Henri and IRIS will help you develop the technologies, but the state of mind depends on you. The screens made their debut and significant changes occurred. If screens arrive at the other globes, you will know that the game is over. Here is the key to your destiny.
4. Act now. Please. They will know everything.
5. You have ten of your years.

Audry disappears; IRIS and Henri smile at all and wait.

Sequestered in other rooms and buildings around the Hague were advisors, chiefs of staff, scientists and first responder teams from Wheeler and NASA. The army, navy and air force were not there, because their toys had all been disabled. They were no longer important.

Het Spaansche Hof (the Spanish Court)

Was built in 1469, it is at 12, 2512 HD den HAAG.

NASA and Wheeler have sequestered the whole place. There are 3D globes, simultaneous translation and a lot of refreshments.

"Damn," said Ludo, "quite a speech, typical Audry."

"And I love what she did with her hair, making it appear on her facial image like that," said Gabriella, without skates but with a big coffee. Meeka agrees and keeps quiet. He likes Audry and she is even cooler now.

"So, we have a chance," says Simone, "that power without pollution thing. There was a material back in 2000, that we were developing, a nano technology, a film that converted infrared into electricity, it would have fixed the energy crisis, but it was unstable and we were having trouble controlling it. I remember

Christophe, a young French designer; he was working on replacement forms of energy for his PhD and managed to get onto our research team as an external. Don't know how the hell he did that, anyway, sharp as a needle and very intuitive. His beautiful, brilliant wife was his rock and constant companion. She was doing research at the Sorbonne, loved chemistry, a hippy at heart. They made a formidable pair. He nagged the hell out of NASA trying to get us to release the information but it became top secret. I wonder what happened to them. I wonder what happened to the research. Perhaps Henri knows."

09.43, The Conference. A summary by the conference leader. Roberto de Suza.

"For fear of making an irreversible decision, we should abandon the summit for the day and come back to tomorrow. This will allow the heads of each country to speak with their advisors, chiefs of staff and come back with a clear mind." She paused and took a sip of water and a deep breath.

"The problem we have is that not all, in fact, only the United States, Russia and China, have experience of the globe effects. Fake news and all that," said Ursula.

"Some chiefs do not believe the globes will affect them, after all, there are only 11 globes in entirety." Another pause. "Those countries that are poor are still poor, but now the Superpowers are no longer super. The biggest problem for all of us is energy production, moving food and materials and controlling people." She continued. "Those who are not affected so far, perhaps think the screens will control people, make them nice and that a form of energy will be provided by the Omnisciences. So, let us have the screens. There will be no planes, but so what? Without crime, free energy, what is not to like?"

Ursula pauses for effect.

"Before we abandon the conference," says the chief of Papua New Guinea, a Commonwealth Kingdom, "we must recognise this, in ten years, without change, the screens will be deployed and that, will be the end. See you tomorrow."

Catch 22

Without the screens, there is no guarantee that everyone will change.

If the screens unfold throughout the world, humanity is dead.

Het Spansche Hof (the Spanish Court)

Mari and her staff managers join Ludo et al at their hotel. Gabriella now carries her skates like a handbag. The carpets were too thick. Roberto de Suza has assumed the role of chairman.

"Let's go straight to it," said Gabriella, taking her chance in the brief interlude of silence.

"Condemned if we do, condemned if we don't. Some choice, Audry!"

"That's true," said Marika, holding a large coffee in her hand and nodding to Gabriella with a wry smile. "If all we have heard is true, humanity is the virus and it will go under its own steam or by the grace of the Omnisciences in ten years. What will remain is a world free of pollution or cruelty to nature and wildlife, with robots as guardians." *Sounds good to me* thought Meeka.

"But we have never been vegetarian, some but not many," said Ludo.

"No," said Marika, "and we could fix that but it is cruelty that will kill us. It's in our nature."

"The Omniscients will fix that," Salvo said. "We can see the evidence. Those that want to look that is."

The room was quiet.

"I think they are playing Poker with us. Maybe, if we manage to change, we can stay here and rebuild our population," says Francoise.

By 11.15 hours, there was no result to the discussions, Marika and the other heads of countries were at a loss. Roberto de Suza cuts through the chatter and asks all to put to him their answers to the following questions by 16.00 hours this afternoon and then for all to come back to the conference at 09.00 tomorrow. It was going to be a long night.

Back in their rooms, refreshed and ready to join up in Marika's suite. Its 6 p.m.

"It's a simple list," said Marika.

"And an impossible list," said Gabriella, "there is no way countries will give up their sovereignty."

"Or have the screens and allow our minds to be modified," says Ludo, "no, we must call their bluff."

It was not a long night for Roberto who decided to take a pill and get some sleep.

21 December The Conference, 09.00 hours

All the responses were sent to Roberto.

It will be a majority vote. The question – **bluff or not?**

There are 206 states of which 193 are members of United Nations organisations, two observers and 11 others.

There are also 16 in dispute. But these will be discounted. 104 is needed to carry the motion or question.

109 voted for a bluff. It's enough.

The motion was carried.

RECORD 5

Gabriella sips her coffee; Meeka is running around. This is the time when humanity grasps a last hope. She thinks carefully about this and what to put in the globe. She considers whether in writing reality, she actually determines it.

She has a point, thinks Meeka.

The Next 10 Years
Year 1, 1 January 2034

Despite the fact that the vote was so tight for the bluff, there was total agreement that the world should continue with the design and building of spaceships. The double bluff.

There are a lot of science fiction ideas that sound pretty but the practicalities are huge and complicated. Many types of competitions were posed but all the solutions had the same problem. How to launch or how to build in space?

The problem sitting behind this was the source of energy and also the materials. Metals and plastics were needed, ergo oil and minerals and therefore the embargo effectively imposed by the Omniscience, makes the task impossible.

Star Date 090.080.647.87. (13).2 Dimension 87. Repair Complex.

Henri's thoughts were communicated to the Omniscient and Audry in complex 87 immediately. Less than a second had passed and already the problems had manifested. The split vote, the resources, the impossibility of the task. There were shortcomings in the Omniscience's plan for humanity and they needed more help to overcome them. Humanity is very resilient and worth sparing. Audry is still human, as little. She will help them.

NASA

NASA has been working on an idea for an intergenerational spacecraft for 20 years, in area 51. The crew will be 100 people. The idea was for it to be built in sections on Earth and assembled in space, like the ISS but it will be very large. Propulsion was a problem that required a lot of development. It is not the case that a spacecraft could realise the terminal velocity, choose a destination and leave it at that. A propulsion system was needed that did not exist at the moment.

The screens were now in place on Wheeler and no flights were possible. Wheeler's key equipment was still on the Gerald R Ford which had escaped just in time. It was decided to bring the Gerald R Ford to NASA and unload the equipment, then send it to an appropriate base. They would head to the naval base in Ventura County, point MUGU, near NASA Jet Propulsion Lab and also LAX. Then, Captain Sam Rodderick would be on a mission.

Jet Propulsion Laboratory Pasadena, California
12 January 09.00 hours
JPL Is the First Facility for Robotic Exploration of the Solar System.

General Ludovic Schmidt, Professor Simone Aubert, Henri and IRIS, were welcomed by General Fletcher, he had only one name and it was always shortened to Fletch. Gabriella was there because she was very smart, with an IQ somewhere well above 173, very funny and anyway, Henri had insisted.

"The task," said Gabriella, with coffee, without skates, but with Meeka close by and having a dog nap, "is to design a material with the power of the Hadron Collider (CERN) without dragging a 17 miles tunnel along with it and without the problems which it had so far experienced and," she paused for effect, "make it small."

"Easy really." Henri smiles, IRIS raises an eyebrow, metaphorically speaking.

Fletcher or Fletch for short was actually short but cut an impressive figure. His hair is blue, his eyes are blue, and his nails are also blue, but he is sharp as a needle. He is also a black American. He smiled warmly at Henri.

"We have a spectacular team here," said Fletch, "the most brilliant brains from around the world, Russian, Japanese, Chinese, French, English, United States of course, sorry if I missed a few. The big news is that we think we found something very interesting, a **wormhole** and we have a robot ready to send. Let me introduce you to the man in charge of the robot and many other things, Masahiko Takao."

Masahiko Takao was very tall for a Japanese at 1.93 metres and very handsome with green eyes, very unusual and yellow hair, quite lustrous, which he wore in the pony tail fashion favoured by the Samurai. He always wears only black and red. Today is black. His birth name is ただ王子と戦士の男 which means (just Prince and Warrior man), but he prefers Benton, which means nothing really.

"Since the deployment of the David Webb telescope on 25 December 2021 (at 12hr 10 minutes) by the Arianspaces ELA-3 in French Guiana, it has been in orbit around the Earth at a point called Lagrange Point (L2) which is 1.5 billion km. from the Earth, having travelled at a velocity of 0.7472kmp/sec for 30 days to get there," says Benton, "and we have been very busy since."

"We discovered the **wormholes** in 2023, but they were immediately classified as **top secret**. There were a lot of secrets then. All the same, there was great scientific cooperation. We found thousands of them. Eventually, we were able to build a device, a portal and now, we can test it."

Benton smiles, beautifully and bows. Henri does the same.

The Portal

"I have to explain something," said Benton, "it's very strange. We had the calculations, the theory, and the portal in a special room ready to go, but we could not make it work. We were in this position for two years, but on 1 January at 18.00 hours, the touch screens came on, the information scrolled down, loads of it, the portal illuminated and a green form appeared. I thought it looked like a person with a big head; others thought it was a triangle, others didn't see anything but all agreed, that the portal was not plugged in."

Gabriella smiles, "It's Audry."

"Who?" Benton said.

The room had the proportions of an aeroplane hangar but was built of concrete and with a concrete roof. It was really a bunker. It was without windows but had large ventilation grilles. The walls shone with soft light, there were hundreds of circles in the ceiling, around 3 metre centres, from which illumination came but there were no visible luminaries. There was a complex of rooms around the hangar with glass sliding doors that retracted in slots. They were opaque but could change colour. At this moment, they are red and at one end there are two huge doors, also concrete, which slide into the walls. In plan, the hanger was surrounded by a 5-metre corridor, golf carts could pass each other easily.

On the other side of the corridor are all the equipment, scientists and technicians and super (Quantum) computers and everything from which information is carried to the touch screens in the hanger. Outside the hangar doors, there was a concrete apron and aeroplane runway with normal facilities. There was no obvious portal but there were two other constructions. One, a large table, 5 metres by 1 metre which was a touch screen and the second, two poles in chrome 1 metre diameter and 7 metres high, 10 metres apart and perforated with small holes of 5 mm. Touch screens are activated by eye recognition only. In the ground, in front of the poles, are chrome discs at around three-metre centres. They extend all the way to the entrance doors, they resemble runway lights. There are no chairs or anything else in the room. It's quiet but disturbing at the same time.

"It takes a little time to get used to," said Benton, with a smile and a bow.

"Is the robot here, and what do you call it?" Simone said.

"It is called ワンソン (Oneson)." ワンソン is a strange creation. It resembles the Michelin man, circular tubes, arms, legs, hands and each tube rotates 360 degrees. The head has a Manga face that is projected on the globe. It is 2.5 metres high, lemon in colour and it has a trick.

"Arrival program please ワンソン," said Benton.

He bows and becomes a ball, still of lemon colour. Then it hovers in the air and the entire globe is a Manga face.

"Smart, don't you think?" Benton said. "It is a form of memory plastic, there are hundreds of programs, and it can change colour or…"

ワンソン it disappeared.

"I need another coffee," said Gabriella as she looked at the mess on the floor.

"I will get you another," said Benton and smiled. A little hemispheric robot appears from the wall, cleans the spilt coffee and cup and returns to the wall. "Follow me, we will go to the laboratory, where we can get more coffee and we need to talk."

They walk towards the red door; it slides into the slot in the wall.

"Do not worry about the golf carts, they will stop automatically."

They entered a corridor; there was a line in the centre. It glowed green. It was 1.5 metres wide.

"We are in green mode at this time, total security. Just stay on the line," Benton says.

There are golf carts and robots of many shapes and sizes everywhere. Some are floating above ground.

They were marched for about 800 metres, as red doors illuminated, carts stopped.

"Is it rush hour?" Gabrielle said, thinking she needed her skates.

"Almost there," said Benton.

The green line became a flashing arrow pointing to the left. What was a red door now indicates the following information in English, French and Japanese.

No. 27
Secure
Biohazard
いいえ 27
牢
バイオハザード

Benton puts his eye on the scanner, red then going green, a whistle and a pair of elevator doors open; they enter and descend to level 9. The elevator doors open.

"We are here," said Benton.

Lab 9

It is a huge space with lines of benches, groups of people in white lab coats, people with ear microphones, and line after storage line with robot parts, legs, arms, torsos, head. In the plan, the benches are arranged in a U form, set on a black square of 3.5 metres, each square is surrounded by a glass wall on three sides. Each edge is bounded by a sidewalk, like a chessboard, but with an entry between each edge. There is a larger sidewalk grid of three metres on the plan and there are nine blocks of benches between the large sidewalks. Golf carts move up and down, piloted by robots, actually, there are more robots than people.

The light is shining on the benches at 700 lux, and less so above the sidewalks, around 400 lux.

"Here, in Lab 27," Benton says, "we assemble the robots, but unlike a production car line, each robot is assembled by hand. You can walk freely; the carts will stop for you. In case of emergency, the golf carts stop immediately on the right in the direction of the evacuation towards the exit. The exits and sidewalks will be illuminated green and there will be an audible alert. You will know if it is an emergency, without a doubt and there is, of course, a random emergency test program. Follow me, gate 6 there, it's a café area and it's restricted access, we could talk there."

They fell in line behind Benton, who walked very fast.

Gabrielle says, "Where are my skates when I need them?"

They all smile. No problem for Meeka.

Room 6

The room is around nine metres square, a pale green table and 10 chairs also in pale green and chrome, sit in the middle.

"Sit down, please, I will order drinks and snacks. You must have a lot of questions," said Benton.

Ludovic, Gabriella, Simone, Fletcher and Henri all take their chairs.

"The first thing," said Ludovic, "is how did you keep all this secret, and does the President know?"

"And what is that floating vision of the Michelin man all about?" Gabriella said. Meeka now adult and very large is constantly by Gabriella's side and is not sure about the Michelin man.

At this moment, the door slides open and the drinks arrive, Benton number 2 wheels in the trolley. A little gasp from everyone as they look from one to the identical other.

"Oneson, I suppose," said Gabriella.

"I'll explain," said Benton 1.

"First of all, Madame President knows, but only since this morning. She is on her way now. Secondly, Oneson ワンソン has been developing its own program improvements, we think courtesy of Audry, so, since 1 January, we have kept silent because we are not sure how or whether to announce the news. Marika, Madame President, is due here by 4.30 p.m. this afternoon. In the meantime, please have a drink and something to eat while we wait."

They all took something from the trolley and settled back in their seats.

There was silence for several minutes.

Henri broke the silence and spoke to Benton 2 in Japanese.

"あなたは多言語の一人です, you are multilingual?"

はいアンリ "Yes, Henri, I am known as Oneson."

"Hi Oneson, please change your clothes," said Gabriella. "It is very confusing."

Benton 2 instantly appears in a yellow shirt with blue pants. "Very funny," says Gabriella, "and thank you." Oneson bows.

"I will summarise," said Benton 1 glancing at Oneson who bows slightly.

1. Oneson can now change shape or form at will, without a program, if the mass is the same or approximately so that is, give or take a few kilos. This was not originally the case.
2. Oneson is of course multilingual. In fact, any language.
3. Oneson is totally sentient.
4. It or he or whatever it is can hear Audry, but can't start the conversation. Henri is helping with that.
5. Oneson has an inexhaustible power cell. It's set at 150 years at the moment, renewable if necessary and it may be, automatically. He will decide.
6. Oneson does not get sick, can self-repair and is effectively indestructible.
7. There is one Oneson, but it is not all of our manufacture and is evolving. Oneson nods and bows slightly and there is a collective intake of breath in the room. Meeka's ears prick up and he looks at Oneson, who nods and smiles at Meeka.
8. If or when Oneson is me, he moves like me, thinks like me but he is not me.

He just is. Oneson.

"So, he is not a clone?" Gabriella says.

"Permit me to explain further," said Oneson, "I may appear like something else, or someone, like Benton, for example, as I am now but I can't be that person. I am, in that guise, a new Benton but not the original and not a clone."

"So, you can take the form of any being or entity at will?" Gabriella said.

Oneson moves to the seat next to Gabriella and looks at her. Gabriella gasps as she looks at herself. Meeka moves to bite Oneson but stops.

"**You** are the new human being," said Gabriella in a flash of incisive brilliance.

"I think so," said Oneson, "as they, humanity are replaced, I become them. There will be many of me."

Oneson bows.

"Cogito ergo sum," says Rene Descartes.

"I quote in Latin," says Simone.

"I think, therefore I am," said Ludo in English.

Oneson or Benton, as he currently appears in yellow and blue morphs instantly back into Michelin man.

He smiles, the whole face and rolls away towards the door and then disappears.

They all look at each other, amused and concerned at the same time.

"How do we know who's who?" Gabriella said frowning.

"You don't, but Oneson will," said Benton "and I will and that is all that really matters now."

"Is it…really?" Gabriella said, not convinced. Neither was Meeka.

Air Force 1

Marika and her chiefs of staff were discussing the news at JPL this morning. She had not communicated with the other leaders of the world and she is considering another difficult discussion with them. Her new assistant, Gerald Sampras 111, not connected to tennis, was tall, and slender with blue eyes, a chiselled face, black hair and a nose like an eagle. Carnegie Mellon University, Pittsburgh, in the first 3 in computer science, very bright, and only 31 years old.

"The robot is called Oneson, Benton's idea," Gerald said.

"I guess he'll look Japanese," Marika said with a smile she did not quite believe.

"On the approach," said Captain Bradley, "it was his father's joke on him, referencing a Leslie Nielson film, quite funny really. Seats and belts, please."

The Motorcade 15.40 Hours

"We take the 105 East and then the 110 North, should take 35 minutes says Gerald. I think that will be met by Benton."

Room 19c 16.53 hrs.

The doors open and Benton enters with Marika and Gerald. It is a room larger than room 6.

"Welcome, Madam President," said Fletcher.

"A little late, the 110, as usual," says Gerald.

"Please sit down, you know everybody," said Fletcher. "Coffee?"

Yes, a collective nod.

The doors slide open with a whistle and Benton enters with a refreshment trolley.

"I'm Oneson," good afternoon all.

"What the ####!" said Marika in one of her rare expletives.

"Oneson, please, change," Benton said with a smile.

Oneson bows and changes into a purple version of Henry and smiles.

"That's better," said Benton.

Silence.

Gabriella as usual was the first to speak.

"Love the new colour, we saw this earlier and I have thought a lot about it since. It is clear that we can't risk sending Oneson into the portal, it is a distinct possibility that Oneson will not return. Also, and this may scare you, if it were possible to create more Oneson's, and no doubt it is, to feel, without violent thoughts, be kind, non-polluting, in contact with nature and so on and allow them to know a particular person, then they, in that guise, will be able to live forever and the Omnisciences would surely be happy with that. But and this is a big but, we would see ourselves getting old and dying. Maybe that's just a little upsetting."

"But if it is possible to do both, live this life here and build our destiny elsewhere, then that might work," said Maila, feeling as if she has solved the problem in Presidential style and pretty damn quick at that.

"It's a plan of sorts," said Benton.

"Maybe," said Oneson (who is still Henri at the moment, but purple of course.)

"Maybe," said Gabriella and Simone in unison.

"Is that the plan then?" Marika said, "The Omniscients solution? To replace humanity with look-alike Onesons and meanwhile, let us struggle to escape. They are punishing us. Do we all agree.?"

The question hangs in the air as they all consider the impact of this scenario.

Then they all smile, Gabriella goes for more coffee; Meeka nips Oneson's ankle, the real Oneson and Oneson and Henri bow together, lemon and purple in perfect unison, a double act; they all laughed.

The Plan

They worked until 20.00 hours, round and round they went.

"That's enough," said Marika, "let's meet again at 09.00, see you tomorrow."

They returned to their rooms, Benton with Henri and IRIS, Oneson was already there, still as Henri in purple. None were smiling.

Room 19c 09.00 a.m., 13 January.

They had coffee, Gabriella had skates and coffee, Ludovic had tea, Marika had water. Benton opened the discussion. Meeka licked his paws.

It is a large room, a lot of space to call other people as necessary.

"There are three things to consider. The things we can do, the things we must not do, and the things we absolutely have to do," said Benton.

The negative first.

1. Do not contact Audry at this time.
2. Do not open the portal yet.
3. Don't tell the world yet, nothing at all, okay? All agree.

Second, the things we can do.

1. Develop a plan B.
    Third, the thing we must do.
2. Identify all those who may be potential space explorers. These will be our hope.
3. Start working on the spacecraft, design and build. Country by country.
4. Make sure we take care of the planet and nature, no exceptions. Nothing left to chance that would push the Omnicients to close the time frame early.

So, plan B, let's get to it. All agree.

Plan B

The complexities of Plan B were huge and ethically complicated. For the first time, IRIS was the first to say something.

"There are three sentient robots here, two of us have been with the Omniciences, Henri and me and one of us is able to become whatever he chooses to be, that's Oneson. Of the others, Madam President, we have Gerald, Ludovic, Benton, Fletcher, Gabriella and Simone. Ten in total to decide the fate of humanity."

"Plus the dog," said Benton. "Audry is no longer human, but she is helping us."

"A good summary, IRIS," said Benton, "let's go."

And so they do.

"The way I see it," said Simone, "it is only the robots that have contact and therefore we rely on and trust them. As for the world, they make their own decision by their actions, but one thing is clear, the spacecraft will give humanity hope."

"It is also clear that it is not possible to build enough spaceships and many will not want to go anyway," says Ludo. "We can develop an algorithm for this. I expect less than half a million."

"Why so few?" Marika said.

"Because of age, health, zero population growth and incredulity. Japan has had zero population growth since 2006," says Benton, "as a result, you could expect the population of the world to be 1.8 billion by 2044, then factor in the algorithm and voila!"

"Also, for those who have chosen to go, they will be indoctrinated by the Omnisciences, and they will be on a spaceship without any idea of when they might arrive somewhere, or if at all. Maybe none will choose to go."

"And there is the question of building spaceships, locations and propulsion systems, all problems of enormous proportions and perhaps, insurmountable even with my help," said Henri. IRIS nods.

"Of course, the ethical question is, what part of humanity do you want to keep?" Gabriella who was now on her skates said. "And if you want it to offer population growth, then generational spaceships are the only way."

"Unless," said Henri, IRIS and Oneson, with a single voice, "you give us your memories."

"That's the real question, that is the real Plan B."

There was a prolonged silence. Benton, Henri, IRIS and Oneson all bow and wait.

Fletcher had thought deeply about the problem. It was clear as crystal to him what they had to do.

"I have a proposal," said Fletcher.

"Please," said Marika.

"It is this. We cannot choose who will live and who will die, therefore, we must put all our energy into the ships and also, send a probe into the wormhole and, it cannot be Oneson. If the probe indicates a habitable world, then we can seize this chance, form a queue to wait and go through and take our chance, but I think the same problem will apply; all people will have been altered by the Omniscient. Only robots will be the same and if we want the essence of humanity to survive, then there is but one choice to make. Who will be Oneson, who will he become."

All look at Fletcher, but it is Marika who answers, "It's clear, there is only one person who can make the choice."

"Audry," They Say With a Singular Voice.

Year 2, 2035
1 January
Madame President of the United States had difficult conversations with other leaders of the world. Populations continue to diminish and 1.8 billion has been predicted by the end of 2044.

There is little criminality as those criminals have simply disappeared. They are not missed.

By 9 July
Henri's gell packs supply machines, transport, electrical networks.

By 18 August
There are now seven spacecraft designs and construction has begun in locations in, the United States, Russia, the UK, France, China, India and Australia. South America and Africa are using the design by Australia. Nine ships in total.

Ambition
Is to build 500 ships by 2041, each capable of holding 3,600 people, assuming that 1.8 million will be sent. It is probable that the final mix of people will be of all ages but the most probable is that the majority will be between 20–45 years.

Each ship will have the same facilities on board. Science Laboratory, World Library, Health, Seed Bank, Wildlife DNA, Food Production, Hospital, Living Accommodation and a team of 100. But all will have a task to do. Other facilitates will be developed as necessary.

Each will also have a necessary feature, a circle that encompasses the ships where the accommodation is located and forms the primary access corridor to all zones. Propulsion is not finalised, but Henri and his teams are working on it.

Each vessel will be self-sufficient.

A program by NASA is used to train the teams.

The plan is to build the ships in sections on Earth and assemble them in space. People will be transported to the spaceships by shuttle which will then remain on the ships.

It's a very great task.

Spaceships have no offensive weaponry but ships can defend themselves automatically.

The Design of Etats-Unis. United States

It is comprised of six sections all the same. A central tube of 180 metres diameter, 30 main bridges, around this a tube of 50 metres diameter with 4 spokes of 15 metres diameter. Further tubes 50 metres long join to the nosecones. These provide the main structural support of the wheel. They are essential for access, circulation, passages, cables, automatic defensive armament, evacuation pods and the drive mechanism for rotation of the wheel. From the four joints with the wheel, parallel with the main body is 4 tubes of 10 metre diameter and 180 metres long. These provide emergency access between the six sections and additional evacuation pods.

The nose cones, 12 of them are the navigation centres 10 metres long, like a jumbo jet at each end. The main body measures 180 metres, so 200 metres with the jumbo extremities. Overall each section is 1,200 metres long by 380 metres in diameter. The front elevation presents the four thrusters, the nacelles, which are located at 45 degrees in each quadrant of the principal body and accessible from the main core.

The outer wheel rotates at 24 cycles per day, counterclockwise. The diameter of the wheel is 380 metres and has a circumference of 1193.05 metres. This provides a reasonable race track of 2 metres wide and no doubt, will become a competition track at some point.

In the case of lost synchronicity of the wheel with the emergency tubes, the double airlock immediately disengages. All components can then be reset later.

Each section is self-sufficient. Overall, the ship is 1.8 km long front first to rear lass nosecone.

Following a critical examination of the design criteria, an additional module for maintenance and spare parts that can be moved from one section to another if necessary was added.

The main problem with the spacecraft developed by the United States at this time is the nacelles and the rotation mechanisms. IRIS and Henri and the technical teams are all working on it. IRIS especially because of her knowledge of transdimensional biscuits.

The pods, the nacelle drives, will work for all six designs.

Henri would like the ship to be lemon. IRIS is not sure. Perhaps pink.

The Design of Royauyme-Uni. United Kingdom

Size about the same as the United States, but the shape is different with common parts. It is in the shape of a funnel in three stages of gradual reduction.

The first reduction is 50 metres, so reduced to (400), the second is 50 so reduced to (300) and the third is 50 so reduced to (200) and then reduced to 180 as in the United States.

The nose cone is 500 metres in diameter, the point of radius is towards the rear of the ship, and the depth is 100 metres. In section, it resembles a large rivet. It has 80 bridges. Behind this is the first wheel 50 metres wide and 600 metres in diameter. In case of emergency, this part, cone and wheel, is uncoupled.

At the other end of the spacecraft, it is the same as the United States with 4 pods 45 degrees each and 4 connection tubes. These provide the main structural support of the wheel and are essential for access, circulation, drives for the outer wheel, passages, cables automatic defensive armament, evacuation pods and the drive mechanism for the rotation of the wheel. This end has 30 bridges.

The wheels rotate in a forward direction and rotate counterclockwise at the rear. There are 24 rotations per day. In the occurrence of lost synchronicity of the wheel with the emergency tubes, the double airlock immediately disengages. All can then be reset later. All as per the United States design.

It seems more spacious than the United States ship and can easily accommodate 1800 people.

Together, the two hold 3600. The rear wheels are connected as the United States with radii of ten metres in diameter in parallel with the main body. The rotations of this ship are reversed so that the rear wheels rotate in the same direction.

The tubes provide access in case of emergency.

Gross square metreage is 10,041,776 per ship = 20,821,532 plus wheels x 2

French Design

As expected, it is different. It is a V-shape with 65-meter-long heels that are parallel to each other and that carry the wheels and nacelles, the propulsion is exactly the same as the United States spacecraft. There are 50 metres between the circumferences of the two wheels.

There are five sections (0,1,2,3,4) all the same, the main body, the V, is 180 metres in diameter, 200 metres long, so 2,000 metres total, 800 metres more than the United States. It is easy to carry the 3,600 people in the main body alone. There are 30 levels or bridges.

In the middle of the V, a 10-meter tube connects the two parts of the V. It is the same access and emergency tube as the United States and contains stores and auxiliary equipment and functions as an emergency access between the five sections and additional evacuation pods, structural stability and automatic self-defence.

It extends from the centre line of the V, each direction by 200 metres. In the middle of each is a double airlock. Centre to centre is 400 metres which makes the size of 5 sections 1980 metres. ($4 \times 400 + 2 \times 190$)

In the plan, the 5 sections look like 2.5 W shape.

Each section has the same navigation deck at the point of the V but the centre section (no 2) will pilot the whole ship. It is hoped that there will be no prima donna drivers. In case of emergency, the five sections are separated and since each function is independent, there will not be a problem.

We do not know the colour but it is hoped to be red, blue and white. It should be pretty.

Russian Design

It's a huge ship. A singular globe diameter of 1000 metres. There are two wheels of 65×180 metres with two wheels of 380 metres, like the France ship.

It is made up of slices of 300 metres centre to centre, like a chocolate orange sweet. The pole caps are 100 metres deep each and home the escape pods, equipment and supplies.

In case of emergency, the floating caps, top and bottom, provide equipment and stores. The globe separates into six slices, each with more escape pods and their own propulsion nacelles. The two heels and their wheels also separate and provide accommodation and essential equipment.

Each slice is self-sufficient and is supplied with self-defence systems. There are 16 decks with an average floor area of about 505,902 square metres each.

From the front on the horizontal axis, it resembles a sliced face with ears and a huge mouth. From above, an egg with the top sliced off and with two wheels on heels on each side. From behind, a globe with two wheels of 380 diameter.

The capacity of all is about 7,200 people max.

In total, there are 32 propulsion systems 4 per slice (6×4) and 8 by the two wheels (4×2).

By comparison, the others, the French have 20, the United States 24 and the United Kingdom 16.

Gross square metre is 48,261,120 (or 1206 large football stadiums of 40,000 each) Plus × 2 wheels. It is twice the size of the United Kingdom ship.

Gabriella pens another note, Oneson is both significant and troubling, and particularly to Meeka and the ship designs are capable of carrying some 50,000 people only. She throws the note at the globe which, as usual, absorbs it and revises the record.

Design Australia

The Australian design has the benefit of being able to see and learn from the other designs of the United States, Russia, the United Kingdom and France.

The Russian ship is very attractive because of its huge size, but it is also the most complicated in case of emergency while the United States is an easy replication of units and more production line than tailor-made. However, the French one is elegant and also of the production line form.

They decided to combine the French with the Russians but with a smaller globe.

The globe is in three sections, but 500 metres in diameter. The top is 125 metres with six decks and a covered dish of 25 metres deep. It is the same as the Russian model which holds the shuttles and pods for emergency evacuation. It has a navigation bridge of 16 metres × 6 metres on the centre horizontal line. At the rear are two nacelle propulsion pods on heels, ten-meter diameter × 30 metre long, common design, centre to centre at 200 metres.

The middle slice is 250 metres with 40 bridges, a navigation bridge, the same 16 metre × 6 metre, two power pods, 300 metres centre to centre on heels at the back.

The bottom slice is 125 metres deep with 20 decks mainly for utilities, food production, hospital, necessary storage, and maintenance facilities for the ship and robots. It also has nacelles and a navigation deck.

The point of difference is mainly that it has an atrium, 350 metres high, 10 metres wide and 350 metres long with elevators, mechanical escalators, shops, leisure areas, cinemas, games, health and fitness, swimming and palm trees. It will no doubt be '**the leisure destination of the fleet**'.

The capacity is 4,000 people.

The colour preferences are green and yellow.

The middle and bottom slices both have, shuttle bays, automatic defence systems and several airlocks and docking ports. The idea is this; in case of emergency, it is always possible to use the vessels and facilities.

Like the Russian design, the three main sections of the globe are all self-sufficient and detachable.

From the front on the horizontal axis, it resembles a sliced face with ears and a huge mouth. From above, an egg with the top sliced and with two wheels in heels on both sides. From behind, a globe with four wheels of 380 diameters.

The capacity of all is about 7,200 people max.

In total, there are 40 propulsion systems. 8 per slice (6×4) 24 total and 16 by the two wheels (4×4).

By comparison to the others, the French has 20, the United States 24 and the United Kingdom 16.

Gross square metre is 48,261,120 (or 1206 large football stadiums of 40,000 each) plus four wheels. It is twice the size of the United Kingdom ship.

The Design of China

Being able to evaluate and learn from the other designs, from the USA, Russia, UK, France and Australia, it is the greatest of all.

It is a globe of the same size as the Australian ship with four main body sections behind which are two huge wheels and below which are four lozenge sections each including four sections 180 square × 200 long. In front elevation, the globe is on the main centre line. The globe is 500 metres in diameter. To the right and left, there are two main bodies the farthest from the globe centre is 590 metres. Below this on a 375-metre vertical centre line is the second ship comprising two lozenges complete with nacelles and wheels.

There is a triangle of radial tubes of 15-metre diameter that connect the two main bodies with the globe and below, another triangle that connects the bottom two ships with the globe.

On side elevation, the ship appears staggered. The top two are equal to the vertical centre of the globe, two to the right and two to the left and the two sections below are three to the right and one left vertical centre of the globe.

Behind the four main sections of the lozenges are the wheels on circular heels, the same as the Australian ship, the standard with four nacelles at 45 degrees.

The globe has two spokes attached to the high section of the globe at 45 degrees which carry the wheels of 380 metre diameter with the four nacelles as normal. The centre of the wheel line and globe is 375 metres. It is symmetrical around the horizontal centre. In total, the ship has six wheels with 14 pods. There is an atrium the same as in Australia.

The size of this vessel is 57,497,600 square metres plus wheels and plus spokes.

The total dimensions of the five components globe (1) plus lozenges (4) are 1280 long × 1000 long plus wheels × 1130 high.

It is the only ship with a square shape for the main core. There are 19 sections in total to that. In case of emergency, each can be dismantled. Each is self-sufficient.

There are 30 decks per 800 metres on the long section, with airlocks, auto defence and escape pods.

The main navigation is by the globe.

It is estimated the full ship can carry 8,500 people max, but China is a large country.

Design India

Versions (1 and 2) **no-go!**

An inelegant and complicated solution and perhaps one with too many problems.

It is a cube of huge dimensions. Four sections each 500×500 metres in plan and 800 metres high. It is very, very big. The inner corner of each block is occupied by an atrium. When all sections are joined, it is the same size as the Chinese design. Each section has a wheel but it needs to rotate on its axis 90 degrees when the entire ship is moving. Calculations indicate that when it is separate, it works well, but as a whole, it will be seriously underpowered.

Not to mention the gross square metreage, there are 133 bridges; the usable area is 133,000,000 or double the Australian spacecraft. There was serious doubt that it was possible to build it in time or at all.

It needs massive change. The size must be reduced and the wheels must be on the opposite side to the direction of travel. Push not pull. It only works as four separate units.

Version 3 (to **go**)

Each cube (4) 400 × 400 × 400 with one wheel each connected by four radial tubes 10 metres in diameter by 20 metres long. In case of emergency, the cubes fall apart and are instantly sealed. The cubes have a 20-metre separation with airlocks. The wheels, as normal, four power pods, a central tube of 180 metres in diameter, and a wheel of 380 metres in diameter.

Each cube has 66 levels of 6 metres approx. height.

With the 66 levels, the gross usable area is 10,560 per cubic × 4 = 42,240,000 square metres, the same as two times the United Kingdom, and so around 7,000 people.

In its combined form, there is a central atrium 20 × 20 metres deep that reduces the usable surface area by 400 square metres. This will be deleted as it gives away too much space.

The ship has the same capability of automatic self-defence, evacuation pods and cargo deck.

The doubt remains if it can be built.

Year 3, 2036

January

The feeling in the United States, having seen the other designs, was that the ships needed more space and an atrium space. The idea to build small units that could join was good but did not make for an exciting trip, perhaps for a lifetime. Marika decides to build a globe the same as the Australian model with three slices, an atrium and six inboard pods.

The fully usable floor size is 11,122,680 square metres and will hold 3,600 people.

The number of people able to travel now is:

United States (2)	3600+4000=7600
United Kingdom	3600
French	3600
Russian	7200
Australian	4000
Chinese	8500
Indian	7000
African	4000
South American	4000

Total 49,500 which represents just 0.0027% of the entire population of 1.8 billion. There would be riots and total chaos.

The portal must work and there must be more of them.

Jet Propulsion Laboratory Pasadena, California

Three years since the conferences in Pasadena, huge progress has been made, especially with energy systems. The gel pack, developed by Henri and his team of scientists, was able to power fusion reactors without the associated problems of nuclear power.

From, cities to cars, aircraft carriers to jumbo jets. It was truly miraculous. In fact, all is ready by the 10-year cut-off. The spacecraft was marketed as an adventure for generations to come.

However, generational spaceships are not like a commuter train and building them is very difficult. Not all countries are able to work at the same pace and there is the problem of assembly in space that requires a space station for each.

It was very clear that the task was more emotional than practical.

Room 19c 11.00 a.m., 15 January.

As usual, Gabriella had skates and coffee; Meeka had her feet, pretending to sleep. Ludovic had tea, Marika had water, Gerald, Henri, IRIS, Benton and Oneson, Ludovic, Simone and Fletcher all took their chairs. For the sake of clarity, Oneson assumes, as usual, the form of Henri in another colour. Today he is orange. Also, he flashes, every now and then a message on his Manga face that simply says Oneson.

"Welcome, Madam President, and everyone," said Benton, "the last three years have been very interesting. First of all, a Nobel Prize for Henri who solved the problem of power, which, in normal circumstances, would save the world."

Applause all around and Henri lights up lemon. Oneson and Benton bow, IRIS lights up pink.

"Like what you have done with the graphic," says Gabriella.

"Thank you," said Fletcher, "and I have an announcement to make."

Everyone turns towards Fletcher.

"We are 65% complete with our spacecraft and we are manufacturing all the wheels and propulsion nacelles for all countries. Our space station is in orbit and in April will accept the first assembly team. In July this year, we start on our globe version. Meanwhile, it is not all good news elsewhere. While the United Kingdom and France are both on the program, Africa and South America are struggling with their construction teams; they are two years behind schedule and need help. India is one year late, Russia and China seem to have very difficult technical problems with their globes and Australia has problems with their construction teams as well but are only six months late, so, not bad."

"Thank you for the summary," says Marika, "I get a slightly different picture when I talk with the chiefs. More upbeat you might say," and smiles.

"All the same," says Fletcher, "we in the United States could solve these problems, but what we can't solve is the numbers. They are very bad."

"It seems to me," said Gabriella, "we have solved the problems the Omnisciences have been concerned about. There is very little crime, no pollution; life is good and rather exciting. The problem now is our declining population which will soon not be able to sustain itself. This is the elephant in the room."

"That's right," says Benton, "because of that we have several things that are now at the top of the list." He summarises.

1. Convince the Omnisciences to change their vision of humanity.
2. Open the portal and build more of them.
3. Or plan B and talk to Audry as we discussed three years ago in this very same place.

"Perhaps," said Simone, "it is their plan, to frighten us to death, to recreate us as robots, no offence intended Oneson and send us off to populate and educate the universe."

There was silence for just a second then all agreed, Benton, IRIS, Oneson and Henri, all bow, again.

"I will call the other chiefs," said Marika.

"I'll speak with Rupert," said Benton.

"Who is Rupert?" They say with a singular voice.

"Ah!" said Benton, "it's complicated, we have something to organise first, speak soon." They apologise and leave.

They needed to expand on what to say and what to do. Time is short. Very short. They instructed Rupert.

Gabriella scribbles some more notes. It's another pivotal point. She tosses the paper at the globe, grabs more coffee and continues writing. She also adjusts the diagrams and calculations for the spacecraft and tosses those in for good measure.

Rupert

Oneson is the most extraordinary entity. Oneson created Rupert because it was necessary to send a probe into the portal and it was clear that it could not be him. Humanity needed an option to their extinction by the Omnisciences and it was clear that spaceships could not solve the problem. Audry must help and with Oneson develops a plan to explore the vortexes created by the portal but she knows that the Omniciences will be watching. Whatever it is that colonises other planets, will not be human in the same form and will not be organic. The spaceships will carry the human organics but they will probably never reach another world and anyway, they will be an adapted species. Adapted before they go. Those who remain on Earth will die out in 90 years. The essence of humanity will be carried by the forms of Oneson, Rupert into other galaxies and as they pass into the vortexes, they will be transformed by the portal. They will be able to replicate and will be immortal but before that, as those humans cross into the portal they will be screened and filtered so that only those suitable, with no defect or evil intent, will be transformed and allowed to travel on. They will begin the colonisation of the galaxies.

But Only Oneson Is Truly Immortal, Omniscient, Omnipotent and Omnipresent.

Ruperts will be the vehicle for transformation, a blank canvas waiting for human data. Their span of life will be thousands of years, but eventually, they will decide to end themselves. 50,000 people will be allowed to travel, the same as those in the spaceships. Those thrown back by the portal will be brought back to Earth to live the remainder of their lives with those who have chosen not to take the adventure.

Eventually, within 90 years, all traces of human existence will have been removed. Screens and robots will remain and will be deployed further to protect animals, mammals, insects, fish and nature itself. The balance of life on Earth will be restored. This will be the new experiment, number 298 and will not be allowed to fail again.

This information is only known by, the Omniscient, Audry, Oneson, IRIS, Henri, the Ruperts and Benton and will always remain only with them.

Room 19c 11.45 a.m., 15 January.

"Welcome back," said Fletcher.

On their return, for a laugh, Henri, Oneson and IRIS all now bear their name tags on their chest and shoulder, in white on lemon, purple and pink.

They all (the three) bow as everyone else comes in, Benton laughs.

"I like what you did with the name tags," said Gabriella, spinning on her skates and finishing with a bow, for which she received a lot of applause and a bark from Meeka.

The doors slide open with a whistle.

Rupert enters, he or she, is androgynous, two metres tall with two big black eyes, hands, feet, arms and legs but without other features, without mouth, ears and nose. In colour, it is mother-of-pearl silver.

"Let me introduce myself," Rupert said to the sound of 'sympathy for the devil' by the Rolling Stones.

"I am Rupert, there will be a lot of me; we serve to accompany those who choose to go into the vortexes and help them in that adventure. Before inviting people to make this decision. For the safety of humanity, I will go first and then report back. It will take me seconds but for you it will be years, I hope four years at most." Rupert bowed and put his hands together in prayer and waited.

Silence in the room, Benton breaks the silence.

"I said it was complicated," Benton said. "The only way to get enough people off the planet, if they want to go, is through the vortexes and we only have one vortex and we haven't tried it yet. Rupert is indestructible; we built him with the help of Audry. He cannot be damaged and he will be back. This is what we tell people, not about the numbers we can evacuate by spaceships as that is clearly, insufficient."

They all agree.

"I will call the other chiefs and offer our help with their problems," said Marika.

"And I'll take Rupert to the vortex," said Benton. "Who will come with us?" Everyone stood up.

The Portal 12.50 Hours, 15 January 2036

Everyone is assembled at the entrance.

The communication globe is connected to all other countries; Benton will give a short speech. Rupert approaches the portal tubes, turns around and says, "Wish me luck. I will be back." There is no music. Rupert disappears.

Star Date 090.080.647.87. 1(3). 5 Dimension 87. Complex of Repairs. The Vortex

There was no tunnel, no speed of light rush, no noise, only a sensation of being stretched to infinite thinness. Instantly, Rupert was next to Audry and instantly, their thoughts were the same.

R: "They will soon be dead, all of them, this must not happen, you must help save more."

A: "This is the maximum I can do at this moment. I will always try to change Omnicient's thoughts and will do so until the end. You must have faith and hope, Rupert. Now there are galaxies to see."

Galaxy Options

A: "There are galaxies in other dimensions that are suitable for humanity to inhabit. Some are very aggressive in their population and in their nature. For these, you will arrive as alien invaders. These will also be potential destinations for spacecraft. Here humanity could be the saviours of the planet, not as was their nature on planet Earth, destroyers."

R: "Will there be weapons?"

A: "No, there won't. When they enter the portal, if they still have some of the traits that were humanity's doom, here they might have a second chance. It is the portals that will decide."

R: "And what of those transformed into Ruperts, the rest of the 50,000, what about those? They do not know they will become robot versions of themselves."

A: "No, they don't and must not know. They will be the terraformers, introduce life, guide it, feed it, and nourish it and then move on to the next galaxy."

R: "How?"

A: "There will be 1,000 Ruperts per planet, 50 planets per galaxy. All that is necessary to develop those planets will be provided, DNA, grains, work stations, accommodation, power, menus from which to choose species of wildlife, mammals, fauna, atmosphere, minerals and of course they will have imagination, a human trait and gift. The Ruperts will be the Gods of that galaxy. In the end, when everything is working, all the equipment will be transferred to the next galaxy. The Ruperts can return at any time to monitor and adjust the balance, as the Omniciences did with planet Earth."

R: "It is easy then."

A: "Maybe, but one more thing, like the cookies or biscuits that you are familiar with from planet Earth you will be able to be in multiple places at a time. So, in reality, and that's what we are dealing with here, there will only be five Ruperts and God."

R: "And who and what is God?"

A: "I think you know. It is time to return to planet Earth. See you soon, Rupert."

R: "Soon, Audry."

The Portal 12.50 Hours, 16 January 2040 Year 7 (Three Years to Go)

In the last four years, a lot has happened.

1. Canada decided to build a spaceship and chose the same as the United States. The United States is helping.
2. India abandon their ships and will wait for the portals or stay.
3. Russia has built another ship the same as the United States with help by the United States and the original design is still in difficulty.

4. Another 0.4 billion people have disappeared worldwide.
5. The world is depressed and civil unrest is on the rise.
6. Benton, IRIS and Henri now communicate without the need to speak.
7. Wildlife continues to thrive.
8. The feeling of people in general is to build the vessels but probably the best thing is to stay on Earth and see what happens. This is a life-threatening condition.

The lights turn red, there is a claxon, all the guards raise their arms and Rupert enters the hanger via the portal that was built at the other end of the floor of discs and opposite the first gate. The discs rise, the space he enters is cased with glass, a ceiling falls on top of him and Rupert is in quarantine.

Welcome again thinks Benton and then remembers to say it.

"Welcome, Rupert," and effects a gentle bow.

"Have a seat while we do some checks."

"And where were you?" Gabriella said with coffee in her hand and skates on her feet.

"Sorry," said Rupert, "I'm a day late."

"Very tardy," said Gabriella and flashed him a smile.

The universe, the 'Milky Way' is in the imagination of the Omniscients. It has existed for 14.5 billion human years. The planet Earth is 4.5 billion years old and for the Omnicients, it is 12 hours. Rupert has travelled for four years, human time, for the Omniscients, this is the same as 0.0000384 seconds.

Rupert looks at his internal clock, it shows 0.0000384 seconds.

"I thought I was faster than that," and laughs.

His experience is already known to Benton, IRIS, Henri and Oneson and they agree on what Rupert should say.

"You look very bright," said Gabriella, "I thought you might be a little dusty."

All laugh.

"Let's start the debrief," said Fletcher, looking very pretty with his blue hair, now his trademark brand, but today with white nails and glasses.

"Are the globes turned off?" Benton said.

"Yes," says security.

All look at Rupert carefully.

"I have been shown many worlds, galaxies and dimensions. There are different solutions for spacecraft and vortexes. First the ships. These are generational vessels and will take some time to arrive at a destination and some may wish to continue on. Some worlds will be hostile and it will be the task of humanity to put them in order. The robots, Ruperts, and Henri will accompany them and provide training for the task and for the maintenance of ships and the necessary equipment on the new worlds. This will be suitable for families and those who are very adventurous, but it will not be easy."

"The second method is by vortexes. These will be established throughout the whole world and like cookies, can be in multiple places at the same time. The portals reassign each of those who have made a mistake and they will stop the passage of animals, wildlife, etc."

"For them, their evacuation from this world is a mission. A mission to terraform new worlds. They will be accompanied by Oneson and the Ruperts, the task is enormous. It won't take any time to travel, that's instant. It is not for the weak heart."

"And the portals will reassign those who are not suitable?" Gabriella said.

"Yes, they will be back in this world in a moment, to continue their lives," says Rupert.

"IRIS will stay on Earth with those who choose to stay and take care of them and Earth's nature and wildlife."

It was a believable speech, optimistic, hopeful, and exciting. Ruppert had done a good job. This is what the world hoped to hear. A benign outcome. But the real truth was something entirely different. The world was not ready for that news.

A deep sense of betrayal is felt between Rupert, IRIS, Benton and Oneson, but that's what they agreed to say. Job done, for now at least and then there's Audry, until the end.

"So," said Gabriella, "there is a plan for the prudent, the adventurous and the totally insane."

"Yes," said Rupert, "that is the plan."

Gabriella had been penning another note, more detailed and it was causing her to take her time. She scribbled away, went for coffee with Meeka and lobbed the note at the globe, which was further away. She thought it wobbled, just for a moment.

2040 Gerald R Ford, 20 January

Since 1 January 2034, Captain Sam Rodderick has been on a mission.

It was always believed that the remote islands would not be affected by the effects of the Omniscient. Other than Wheeler, there were no screens.

According to whether women on certain islands were pregnant. Captain Sam Rodderick's mission was to go to these islands, take some of them on board the carrier and then search for the common factor of their genetic form. If it was possible to reproduce because of a genetic quirk, then humanity was not finished.

The best scientists of the genetic engineering fields have been seconded on board the Gerald R Ford, Regulus Theraputice (founded 2007), Tessera Therapeutics (founded 2020 USA) Takeda Pharmaceuticals (founded 1781 Japan), Sixfold Bioscience (founded 2017 UK), Sangamo Therapeutics (founded 1995 USA) and Pfizer (founded 1849 USA).

In addition, onboard are complete medical facilities, doctors, psychologists, and teachers. The leader of the project is Dr Abe Ito (Abe-peace Ito-The One), 1.93 metres tall with black hair in the manner of the Samurai and green eyes, which is very unusual. He has been a friend of Benton since his childhood. He is 27 years old.

The first port to call was Tuvalu, which was sinking and had a population of around 11,000. There are some Japanese families, their origins from the Second World War.

Two young families were invited on board, initial analysis indicates both have an IQ of at least 165, and children, both 10 months old and speak Japanese and Polynesian.

Other Polynesian Islands have also been visited; Tonga, Fiji, Pitcairn, Samoa, Cook and so on throughout the South Pacific. So far, 36 families with 93 young children and babies and all initial analysis is the same. IQ, bilingual at the age of ten months. The ages of adults were between 19 and 28 years when they were picked up. The youngest adult woman and mother is a computer science teacher now 23 years old with an IQ of 190 and is helping with research.

Sam Rodderick and the most precious cargo ship is now on its way to Sri Lanka via New Zealand and Tasmania. The immediate plan is to meet with the carriers of other countries in Mauritius in April. This will be the largest assembly of aircraft carriers, but without their aircraft, since the Second World War.

There are other common characteristics. The most striking is the green eyes, their height is greater than average for their age, they are all vegetarian and adults and those 10 plus all speak Japanese, English, French, Arabic and Indian, five languages plus their native plus another that varies between German and Spanish. None have ever been sick, all are athletic, all ambidextrous and all love wildlife.

What is not known, by the others on board, is that they can all communicate with each other, without speaking in any language.

10.36 a.m. the White House.

Marika, the Joint Chiefs of Staff and Gerald are all clustered around the globe, coffee and colourful clothing exposed. Not too much decorum this morning in the White House.

The globe illuminates.

"Good morning, Madam President and all, if I may say so, very colourful this morning, Marika."

"Thank you, Sam, what news?"

"For once, the news is good."

"Then, let's have it."

"Well, in addition to what you already know, the IQ, languages, eyes etc., they are all orphans, those we have on board and those we left, also, their genes have been manipulated, 46 chromosomes in pairs of 23 each as normal, but different. The consensus is that they are a new species of humanity, not an evolution of it. The oldest, who is now 27 years old, but seems a teenager is known to others as 伊藤 阿部 the one, Abe Ito. And another thing, in a rigorously controlled test, if we show them a location on a map or a random number, say 396601 to one of them, all know. We have run this test a hundred times; it never fails."

"That's all?" Gerald said with a laugh.

"There is something…"

"What?" Marika said.

"They don't need to talk, they are telepathic."

A silence.

"And how are they?" Marika said, having another coffee.

"Well, they are all really interested in experiments and have designed new experiments, which did not occur to us. They also heal very quickly."

"Did you discuss Part 2 of the experiments with them?" Gerald said.

"You mean Africa?"

"No, we think we have to wait until the rendezvous with the other carrier group in Sri Lanka in April."

"I expect you won't be able to keep it a secret until April," said Marika. "That's all?"

"Yes, that's all for now but contact me if you have more news."

The globe went blank.

"Well, as we thought then."

US Space Station 25 January 2040, the Karman Line 62 Miles Over Planet Earth.

The station is really huge. It looks like a cake stand. A central pole 10 metres in diameter connects five saucers. The top and bottom are 150 metres apart and the two middle accommodations are 300 metres, 900 metres total high. The accommodation saucers are 500 diameter and 10 metres deep with 20 plexiglass domes each top and bottom.

The accommodation is well-lit and spacious.

The high saucer is command and control, positional thrusters and antennas, the bottom is arrivals and departures, very much like an airport. Below is a net for storage and sorting and under this, solar panels. The net is one square km. The shuttles with the pre-assembly parts arrive at the net and wait to have their position on the stand confirmed. It is very busy but very well organised.

There are nine assembly ports, one per country. The Indian wharf is empty but will hold the globe of the United States.

Most assembly is done by robots but some tasks need the human touch in spacesuits.

All spaceships are almost finished and are running functionality tests. The whole operation was an example of the best cooperation in the world.

The plan is to start training and acclimating people and crews now and tease out any problems before the launch in 2043. It is expected that there will be many problems.

Zambia, Africa, 26 January 2040.

Zambia is enclosed by Tanzania, Malawi, Mozambique, Botswana, Namibia, Angola, Zimbabwe and the Democratic Republic of the Congo. The Kalahari basin starts from the Kalahari Desert. It borders Zambia in the south with Botswana. People are called the San, hunter-gatherers, now dying. The desert is 350,000 square miles.

The great arrogance, the idea, is to build a complex of geodesic domes around Mongo, from where the 'green eyes, as they are affectionately called', will begin to develop their projects. Other green eyes will go to Ethiopia; the birthplace of humanity and then repopulate the world as the existing species gradually disappears. Or maybe, they will decide not to get bogged down in the world's problems and join the queues waiting to enter the vortex, or return to the place where they came from, or do something completely different. Someone should ask them.

Meanwhile, the domes are under construction and there is a lot of excitement about the project that is bringing employment to the region, one of the poorest in the world.

April

The complex is complete, it covers an area of ten hectares, laboratories, accommodation, solar energy panels and Henri's gel packs and there is a large lake. It is very beautiful and wildlife approaches with interest.

Gerald R Ford, About Mauritius, 19 April 2040, 17.30 Hours (7.30 Washington)

It is a great assemblage of supporting ships, aircraft carriers and craft. Very beautiful!

In the conference room, Captain Sam Rodderick hosts the nine captains of the other aircraft carriers. Abe Ito is here and the globe is on.

"Hello everyone," and, "Hello again, Abe, it's wonderful to see you," said Marika, "what's the weather like?"

"It's very beautiful, Madam President. Sam, would you like an update?"

"Yes, if you like."

"Well then, the first thing is that we have on board the nine ships 2879 volunteers and there are three pregnant women at the moment and everyone is very excited. But, there is concern and it is very easy to see why."

"Continue," Says Marika.

"Well, they all know that they are different but do not want to be seen as 'the freaks' but more important is that they think the Omniscient recognise this and will apply the same conditions to them because they are not sure how the babies will develop if they send them through the portals. They are determined to erase humanity on planet Earth and so we have three years here and then, we have to go. We are all here have the same feeling, including Oneson, Benton, IRIS and Henri."

"Is it true, Abe Ito?" Marika said.

"Yes," said Abe Ito, "but there are reasons to be hopeful, well two actually. One is Audry and the other is that we will be able to return in about 90 years."

"You mean once those on Earth have all died," said Marika.

"Yes, Madam President, we will be back but as aliens."

RECORD 6 DEPARTURES 20 April 2043, the 9 Spaceships.

To choose Independence Day for a massive departure from planet Earth does not seem appropriate and therefore a random date was chosen.

There were parties but no fireworks.

All the leaders of the countries decided to stay but the ships were full, 49,500 people, including crew, robots and more than 500 green eyes.

The selection process was serious with psychoanalysis, health, aptitude and intelligence tests and evaluations plus rigorous training on board. This took three years and there were many rejections. It is fair to say that each ship carries an elite team. All the Captains were Astronauts. Henri is with the ships of the United States, which are all called, USS Voyager 0-9, 0-9.1–0-9.5 for the 6 parts and the globe is called USS Independence. Also on board is Gabriella Marinello with skates and Meeka.

Gerald Fletcher, Simone Aubert, Ludo Schmidt, Frederica Buscomi, Ralph Van Neames, Livia Bianchi, Brendon Murphy, Rene Suchet, Lucien Palmer, Mads Olsen, Salvo Bartoli, Francois Dupont, Brad Smith and Abe Ito. Gerald Sampras 111 chose to stay with Marika and IRIS is at NASA. Benton, Oneson and Rupert are in Pasadena.

The James Webb Telescope (2020) identified many of the ancient galaxies but it took a month to arrive at 'Lagrange Point 2' to travel at 2,230 mph. The Parker Solar Probe (2018) took 90 days to reach the sun at a velocity of 430,000 mph, which is 0.064% the speed of light. (186,000 mps, 300,000 kps).

Rupert had received information about the planets with existing life, perhaps hostile, or which could be habitable once terraformed, as destinations but the distances are enormous and consequently if the exodus travel time from planet Earth is not to be endless, the mission will need to develop a capacity to travel faster than the speed of light. Or not and maybe back to planet Earth in 90 years. It's a good plan. IRIS loves it, One son loves it, Rupert, Benton, Abe Ito and Audry all love it, although the idea of terraforming other planets via portals seems more attractive to Benton, Audry, Rupert and One son, but no problem, first things first.

Meanwhile, the focus of the activities of Henri and the other scientists and green eyes is to develop a light drive that involves changing space, like portals, rather than designing a very powerful and totally insane gel pack for nacelles. This will be under their control while the portals are controlled by the Omniscients. It's a coincidence because Omniscients may not like it. That's life!

20 May 2043

Life on board the USS Voyager 0-9 had settled into a routine. They have a star clock, calculated and synchronised by Henri and also their 24-hour clock. The spaceship works like a sea ship and Sam Rodderick was very helpful in establishing this. The problem was who was responsible. The choice was easy, the captain was Henri.

The composition of the ship.

Head of Mission, Henri.

- Commander and First Officer Abe Ito.
- The third commanding was the first from the astronauts Captain Stephanie Miller and then lieutenant-commander Randle Simms 11, and Buzz Conke, who was second to none.
- There is no fourth level of command but in case of disaster, the robots will take command with Henri.

The spaceships each had a different number of pods. All are capable of separation in case of emergency and therefore their configuration when combined affects the number of nacelles that can be used.

The numbers of nacelles are United States USS Voyager 24, USS Independence 16, United Kingdom 16, France 20, Russia 24, Australia 40, China 24, South America and Africa are the same ship as Australia.

India did not succeed in making their ship but the United States built another globe.

The fastest ship of the nine is the French, capable, it is estimated, of 450,000 mph, the slowest is the Voyager 0-9.1>0-9.5 because of the vortex due to its linear alignment, but if separate they are the same as the French. The next slowest is the ship of United Kingdom for the same reason as Voyager but, like the United States, it is the same as the French when separated.

The Chinese spacecraft is also very fast and perhaps the fastest because of the number of pods but the estimate is not yet verified and the Australian type with 40 pods that have not been tested either is perhaps the 'Usain Bolt' of them all.

The mean mission speed is 300,000 mph. which accommodates the fastest and slowest ships.

Life on board the USS Independence which is the USS Globe, 5 miles behind the Voyager 0-9 complex, is the most hectic because this is where the light propulsion experiments are taking place.

30 May, Separation Test

Once a month, one of the vessels runs an emergency test. This will be the first separation and it will be Voyager. In case of malfunction, the Voyager 0-9.1>0-9.5 will be the only problem for the mission fleet.

08.00 hrs. (ground mission time)

"Release the inertial locks," says Stephanie Miller, the captain of Voyager 09.

Stephanie is a Texan with an English father; she is tall and thin with grey eyes and short black hair.

The double airlock closes, all interconnection services are cut, and the ship is free.

"Engage thrusters for manoeuvring, a quarter speed."

"Free," said co-pilot Vincent Chu, "and manoeuvring at one-quarter speed to the left and holds at 1 mile."

Ditto Voyager 0-9.2

Ditto. 0-9.3

Ditto. 0-9.4

And finally, 0-9.5 is free as it was separated by 0-9.4. The line is somewhat straggly diagonal as it was necessary to adjust speed a little. Shape is not as important as a clear separation.

And then the screens in 0-9.5 go red.

"Airlock fault," says Joe Ford111, captain of Voyager 0-9.5 Joe is a former F35 pilot who transferred to the astronaut program in 2040.

The two exterior and interior locks had not engaged completely and the air pressure was escaping.

But the systems are very good, a team wearing spacesuits is already on hand and the escape is contained in nine minutes. No problem, but a big warning.

As part of the exercise, the other eight ships automatically sent their shuttles and two teams in spacesuits, to inspect the outer seal of the airlock to Voyager 0-9.5. They find a small piece of neoprene floating next to it. They decide to reopen the airlock and carry out a repair to the neoprene. It took 15 minutes, the airlock was reset and all was ok. A sigh of relief all around.

The initial idea was to carry out one test per month but in light of the Voyager 0-9.1>5 problem. It was decided to carry out three tests per month. That said, there's a saying, *If it's not broken, don't fix it*. Someone should have listened to that.

10 June second separation test, the Chinese spaceship.

It was a near disaster. It is very complicated with a globe, four lozenge sections and six wheels.

The globe captain is Chih-Cheng 是志成; he is 29 years old and pilots the globe. Jaio-long 饶龙 (scaled dragon) is 31 years old, Li Jie 李杰 (beautiful hero); he is 26, very handsome and Jia Li 李佳 (good and beautiful) is actually very beautiful and finally, Nuwa 女岚 (creator of the whole universe) and she is remarkably tall at 1.93 metres and exceptionally beautiful, she is 27 years old.

The first problem occurs with the 15-metres diameter triangle of tubes that connects the globe to lozenge number 4 port sides.

"What is the problem?" Jai-Long says. "I have a red screen but no other information. No text…a break."

"I had a report of a fracture in the tube next to Lozenge 4 and 3," said Jai-Li, small but mean.

"OK…Stop all disassembly at this time and wait for further instructions."

"Meet me there in five minutes. Nuwa, you have the com."

When Jai-Li arrived, the repair and Jai-Long teams were already there.

The crack was some 2.5 metres long but not at the junction, it was in the tube.

"Send the teams to check all the tubes in all the ships," says Jai-Long just as the other shuttles arrive at the loading dock of the globe.

The tubes are not only purely structural but also the primary access between the ships.

"Let me know as soon as you have more information," says Jai-Long, "I will be in the globe."

Chih-Cheng decides to call all the other ships and recommends a check. All the comms globes went live.

All construction information is digital, including structural integrity and testing of welds. The crack is in the tube circumference welds, not the tube itself. It took 15 hours to check all the welds and there are 28 small cracks in total. About 1–1.5 metres.

The automatic sensors only pick up the large crack of 2.5 metres, not the smallest, which is another problem that needs urgent action.

"There is good news and bad news," said Henri to Chih-Cheng.

"The good news is that we can fix it," says Henri.

"And the bad news," said Chih-Cheng.

"Is that it is probably sabotage."

"What?" Chih-Cheng said. "It's not possible, everyone on board this spaceship was vetted, very carefully, it's just not possible. Are you saying the ship is self-destructive in some way, inherently flawed?"

"Well, here is the thing," says Henri. "The welds were ok when the ship was built and all were checked before our departure, so, as a result of this, since fractures are a result of stress and we checked the components in question and they are not under stress naturally, so, they were stressed since our departure. The question is, how? And why?"

"Well, we can't keep it silent, the welds that is, but we can keep our suspicions quiet for now, and in fact, we must," Chih-Cheng said. "What do you think, Henri?"

"It's perverse, but I wonder maybe if it's an ancient vendetta?"

"What for?"

"Well, something to do with COVID, Wuhan in 2020, the Chinese people, everyone is suffering and for a long time. It could be anyone or anything," says Henri.

"In fact, there is a very disturbing possibility and that is that one of the robots was programmed, before the mission began, to damage or destroy the complete Chinese spaceship and the robots are indestructible...This problem may be impossible to solve."

Henry bowed and waited. Chih-Cheng was in deep thought, after several moments he looked at Henri.

"Henri, we must make an announcement and we must make a plan. As head of the mission, the two tasks are yours to do."

Henri addresses the globe. All the vessels are watching.

"You seem very lemon this day," said Gabriella, "how was your little trip to China and what the news is?" Henri's smile is, as always, brilliant but Gabriella sensed a concern.

"The problem is a defect in the welds, as you all know, there are 28 cracks in total in the range of 1–2.5 metres, and all are being repaired now. What is puzzling is why because the tubes are not stressed and the records demonstrate that they were ok before departure. So, something caused the failure in flight and we have to find out what that is. We have a team of robots with sensors to check all the tubes in all spacecraft and they will report to me directly. So, I will report again...stay tuned to this channel says Henri with his widest smile and his brightest lemon colour none of which he really felt was appropriate."

"The bigger problem for the mission is that all the systems are controlled by robots and so it may be that the information is false, there are no cracks or there are others that are not found by the systems." Henri decided to search for the cracks by humans and that it should be a part of their daily routine.

Meanwhile, there is the light-speed propulsion system to resolve and the other spacecraft tests and separations to undertake. Where is Rupert when you need him?

Book 6 April/May 2043, the Portals

Since 20 April and the grand departure, two things have happened. The first is the method for use of the portals and the second is the fear of people to do so.

The organisation was enormous, the questionnaire, the psychoanalysis, the decision to go and then departure details, days, time and places specific to the whole world and in numbers which were limited to 500 per departure…The process was ongoing for three years before 2043 and the boarding gates look like aircraft terminals. Departure gates have been added to existing terminals, for example, LAX, LHR etc. etc. so that on arrival with the departure ticket in hand, you go to gate 4 for Paris or gate 2043 for outside the world. All terminals, new and existing additions, have the same things in common. They are globes with only one sign, an emogee of a man, a woman, a child and a robot, all holding hands, with a background of stars.

Inside the globes are a series of rooms with chairs like an aeroplane seat but with a harness like a racing car driver.

Within the globe, the rooms are as follows.

1. A Reception, this room is semi-circular, 20 metres wide by 10 metres deep. Three doors at the entrance slide open, 10 people at a time, are greeted by two robots that are standing at a reception, a glass lectern, on which appear their details. Once checked, the robot asks the person to present the back of their hand. The robot touches it and they are invited to the next room which is a circular corridor 30 metres wide by 20 metres deep.

2. A the corridor, circular, there are four sliding doors and in the hallway are changing rooms and toilets. There is a robot in each room.

The corridor is translucent and there is background music. Each changing room is very spacious, translucent and with a large mirror, lemon-coloured fabric sofa and a glass table on which is a one-piece suit in a soft grey material for each person. Instructions by the robot are to remove all clothes and jewellery and place them in the numbered box. Single people and those with families all go through to the cabins.

Families with children are all in the same cabin at the same time. There are two sliding doors to the cloakroom, entrance and exit. **It is here that the choices are made.**

If there is a family with children and parents that are not clear to go because of their previous nature or acts, then the parents are guided through the exit door, where they will be transformed into an animal or species that was previously extinct and live happily ever after as such on Earth. If the child or children are pure, then they will be adopted and protected by a robot and will not remember that they had parents and the other passengers will not notice anyone missing, but the robot sheds an electric tear and the total numbers for this trip are adjusted.

Every single person who is not allowed to go through by virtue of their nature or acts is transformed in the same way and forgotten.

3.   A. B. C. D. Flights

These look like the interior of an Airbus A 380 with two decks each capable of carrying the max of 125 people in four cabins. A total of 500 people.

Dimensions are 73 metres long and seven metres in diameter.

The seats are large each with their harness and covered in a coloured fabric of lemon, red and green and each with a screen in the back of the front seat.

There is a grey floor and the back of the seats are also grey. There are overhead lockers that contain the numbered boxes. There are two islands and three banks of seats in form 2.4.2. on the upper port and 3.5.3 in the middle. There is a storage space of 1 metre underneath. In the middle of the tube is a spiral staircase of two-metre diameter and there are robot stations at the front, around the spiral and at the end of the tube there is also a large screen.

Everyone was seated; the Ruperts were moving up and down to check the harnesses. There was a blip, blip.

"Welcome all," said Rupert 1, "there are ten of us with you on the journey. Please listen carefully to this announcement."

Rupert smiles, bows and shines lemon. Children laugh, people smile back.

"You are all here because of your own choice; you represent the best of humanity. This trip is a journey in a way, it will take, but a few moments but on your arrival, thousands of years will have passed here. There is no return; all that you know will no longer exist. I will explain what will happen next and after that, if you are not sure, you can leave through the door at the back. Everything will be as you left it."

"All good? Then this is what will happen next." There was a brief pause before Rupert continued.

"The light will dim, a scan at the molecular level, will start from the back of the ship and travel up the cabin. This will take about 15 minutes, after which we, Ruperts (1–10) will serve you drinks and breakfast. This will take about 30 minutes, you can go to the toilet, they are situated at the front behind the screens and relax or walk as you wish and in the meantime, your information will be processed before departure. You may be wondering what will happen to you. It's complex and very exciting."

"You will be augmented and you will have evolved, your IQ, your abilities, your lifespan and you will be able to realise your dreams, a surgeon, a gardener, a philosopher, engineer, anything at all but there is a central task which is to terraform the planet and therefore, you will all be explorers. On arrival, you will find a complex of geodesic domes in which you will find all you need. In total, we anticipate a population of about 50,000 people. The technologies there are beyond your dreams but it will be difficult. You will have no offensive capability in case of emergency or attack by aliens but you will have defence weapons and the Ruperts and the domes are armoured. The new world is about the same size as this planet."

"The last to arrive will be the mission leaders, Oneson and Benton and maybe some green eyes. Your eyes will have changed also to green. Does anyone want to leave?" Rupert 1 said.

Another thing, all of you will speak the same language.

Three individuals and one family of five raise their hands and leave through the door at the cabin entrance which now says Earth 2043.

"We will now collect your trays and check your harness, then, the light will fade and you will feel as if you are floating and we will have left to start a new life. Good luck to you all."

White House, 30 May 2043, 21.30 Hours.

Marika, Gerald and IRIS were sitting in the Oval Office. She raises her glass, IRIS bows her head.

"Well, this is the time for us and humanity, we have all played our cards, the spaceships are on their journey and another 49,000 augmented humans have started their journey with Benton and Oneson and the Ruperts. For us, their journey will take thousands of years, for them, a few seconds. God bless them. Humanity on Earth will all die in two generations. Another toast then, to your health."

"You know that certain recently extinct species are back, (Poison Frog, 2020 Spix's Macaw, Northern white rhinoceros 2018, Baiji 2017, Pyrenean Ibex 2000, western black rhinoceros 2006) hundreds of them, it's wonderful," says Gerald, "I have a list here."

"It is the Omniscient," says IRIS, "and it will continue and I will remain with humanity until their end. Then I will join Benton and Oneson. The robots will stay here with the animals and wildlife and they will never be destroyed again."

Gabriella wrote a very long note, it was optimistic and filled her with joy and Meeka liked it too.
She went for coffee; Meeka in tow, the globe was quite a way off. She wondered about that as the notes were absorbed and the numbers momentarily appeared.

Book 5, The Journey
Year 1

There were five new people on board the USS Voyager 09 and 2 in 09-3, all babies with green eyes.

The rota of tests continues with great success over a three-month rotation, Vostov 4 (востоков) from Russia, Madame Juliette from France, Boomerang from Australia and the same design Zulu from Africa and Beautiful Forest (Pratige Bos) from South America.

The remainder of the fleet comprises the United Kingdom, Arc Royal 6 and the USA, with 2 ships, USS Voyager 09-1-5 and USS Independence, but Lie-Long 美丽的 (Beautiful Dragon), the Chinese ship continues to be plagued by problems.

Henri and his team continue to work on the light-speed drive while fighting against the sabotage on Lie-Long.

Minor disagreements occur but are quickly forgotten.

By December, the celebrations for Christmas are underway and life on board the ships seems good.

Year 2 2044, and the year of 木 鼠 wood rat in February.

The New Year celebrations on 31 December/January 1 included a lot of singing, there was no alcohol on board, but there were some very special cakes and a lot of travel between spaceships. The robots all wore large jester hats and Henri was spectacular in his red and white polka dot pants flashing in harmony and with his lemon face, which was also flashing with the numbers 2044. He looked very pretty. They visit the other ships and Gabriella accompanies him with skates which are also flashing and delivers cake with the number 2044 also flashing. The Australians had their barbeques and the 'Brits' sang 'Auld Langsyne'.

Work is progressing on the Chinese non-explosive fireworks.

The leaders of each spaceship had decided that from this year forward, a meeting once a month on a rotation basis would be a good idea. Today, 1 February, all are on the USS Independence.

"Welcome all to USS Independence," said Gabriella with skates and coffee and Meeka, who seems a little agitated. "There is no agenda but there are some problems, maybe we can find some solutions."

"D'accord," says Simone Aubert.

"Well, we have a big problem," says Vincent Chu, co-pilot of USS Voyager, "and it is that our 'cheerleaders' refuse to wear their flashing skirts."

A brief silence then bursts of laughter, Gabriella spills her coffee, then nacelle number 4 in wheel 6 escapes from the Chinese ship together with a cloud of green smoke resembling a dragon and on board the spaceship on all screens, 'Happy New Year, Wood Rat 新年快乐木鼠.'

Within seconds, repair teams were mobilised, including the Chinese, the United States and the United Kingdom.

Head of China's Jai-Li, USA Bradley W Bush 11 and GB, Michael Norris plus robots and spacewalkers. The nacelle was floating about 150 metres from the wheel and moving away. Three robots with jet packs and grappling hooks were in hot pursuit. All the information appears on the screens on board the shuttles.

"And a good year to you, wood rat, what a mess," said Jai-Li, "this is an explosion, not a structural failure."

The four spokes of the support were in pieces and floating slowly away, four holes with jagged edges pointing outwards were visible. The robots secure the nacelle and return to the Lie-Long (Chinese ship).

"This must have happened before we left the Earth," said Bradley, "it is sabotage."

"You mean the explosives were already there?" Jai-Li said.

"Exactly," said Bradley, "and this is good news, in a way, but also very worrying."

"Why?" Jai-Li says.

"Because we couldn't discover the explosives and we have been looking for sabotage since the fractures," Bradley said. "Well, Henri and his team had."

"It's not common knowledge," Michael said in his clipped accent.

"No, it's not," said Bradly, "and probably, if possible, should stay so."

The teams stay on station for another three hours to make more checks, but after that, return to their own ships as new parts must be manufactured.

Independence 2 February, 10.30 Hours

All the old team from Pasadena were there plus all the leaders of the other ship; the news of sabotage was out.

Henri begins his briefing.

"Welcome aboard USS Independence, everyone. It is now clear that there was a plot to destroy the Chinese ship and this was planned before our departure. It did not cause us huge harm, thankfully, but it's serious. So far, our robots have not been able to find out what the problem is and yet, we have them. I am open to suggestions."

Abebe (lemand wat afwyk) (the one who wards off) is two metres high and looks very handsome wearing a jumpsuit of several colours.

"I'm available for booking for special occasions," Abebe said with a big smile while pointing to his suit. "We have the same ship as Australia and South America and we do not anticipate any problems, but other problems may arise so we need an emergency plan."

"And what could it be?" Gabriella said, coffee in hand, skates on her feet, a smile on her face and a Meeka in fine shape, wagging his tail.

"Well, an evacuation plan, to begin with, a good plan and not a panic plan and we need to rehearse it in place of the separation tests, perhaps," says Simone Aubert.

"Or, as Gerald Fletcher says, we may have to change parts."

"Cannibalise you mean," said Abebe, "We are good at this!" with an even wider smile.

Henri bowed and everyone smiled.

For some time, Henri had been communicating with Meeka without speaking and Meeka was changing.

Madame Juliet, 10 February

The day of the separation test and also the first component exchange.

It was decided to exchange pods 4 with 1 and to swap the pods 2 and 3.

"So far so good," said Francoise la Blanc, captain of the French vessel as the first separation was made. The airlocks work very well on the 15-metre diameter links.

The next exercise was to disengage nacelles 2 and 3. She took a deep breath and signalled to begin the operation. There are four nacelles per wheel. The first of the four separates easily, ditto the second and the third.

"Number 4 will not move," says Henrie Messier, shuttle pilot of the MJ4. "Automatic release is offline."

"We'll reboot and try again," said Francoise.

"Okay," said Henrie.

After the fourth attempt, they decide to separate the nacelle manually. Two other shuttles are on station, the robots get to work and after 30 minutes, the nacelles are free.

"Very well," said Francoise, "now cross your fingers."

The exchange involves the same procedure for nacelle3. Disengage the nacelles, and then exchange them with two on the other wheel. It is a disaster. The four nacelles explode when the automatic release is triggered and hit the 50-meter diameter wheel, there are severe casualties, 20 people dead and 49 injured. Alarms can be heard in all other ships.

Emergency systems work very well, with airlocks every 25 metres and robots medically capable of capturing those in sections without pressure suits, but there are body parts and floating bodies and the carnage is terrible. In minutes, the shuttles of the other ships are on hand and with excellent triage, the emergency is under control in three hours. The consequences are more difficult to solve. Dr Rene Delacroix is the Chief of Medical Services.

All the leaders of the spacecraft and the original Wheeler team leaders were assembled in the atrium of the Chinese globe.

"I wish the circumstances were better," said Rene, "I want to give you an update and discuss what to do with the dead. First, there is some good news. Those with missing limbs are in intensive care but will be equipped with cyborg limbs and other body parts and make a complete recovery, except those who do not have a head, we can't do that."

"And you don't think that's a strange thing to say?" Gabriella said.

"Well, we could but shouldn't, that's the point."

"And there's a choice of colour?" Gabriella said, trying to lighten the mood.

"Of course," said Rene, still oblivious to the black comedy in what she said.

Henri smiles and taps on his head which flashes lemon and everyone smiles, job done.

"I suggest that we do a numbers check, asap, dead, injured from everyone. Maybe we should freeze the bodies for burial in space or cremate them and wait until we get to our new home. Please take views on this and let me know."

"It's a Rumsfeld moment," said Henri. "We know that we have a saboteur and we know we have four destroyed pods. What we don't know is if the pods were sabotaged or if it was a failure of equipment. Both are problematic."

"Why?" Ludovic said. "We have the spares, we can fix them."

"The problem," says Henri, "is that we do not know if the spares are ok and we do not know if the saboteur or saboteurs are on board."

"What's the plan?" Gabriella said.

"I suggest that we establish a police force," says Brendan O'Brien, "and Mike Prentis can re-establish the Dallas scanner team."

"It is strange how it is that this new society soon needs the attributes of the old," says Gerald Fletcher.

"Yes," said Gabriella, "but at least we don't have taxes."

"We will need uniforms," said Ludovic.

"And so on and so on," says Gabriella, "before we know it, we will have a replica of society on Earth, what a pity."

It was agreed by all to create a Space Security Council with Abe Ito as head. A good reason for this is the green eyes do not need to talk to each other. This would increase security and also, they are the best equipped, other than Henri, to deal with the robots.

Independence, 15 February

Brendan, Henri, Mike Prentis, Abe Ito and Gabriella, were all in conference room 03 which had a large atrium. People, robots all milling around, the noise and hustle and bustle of normal life.

Meeka was very busy hunting robots.

"I thought about a possible scenario that explains the situation if that's what it is," said Abe, looking serious but with smiling eyes.

"And?" Gabriella said wearing skates and coffee was her regular habit.

"Well, on 24 February 2022, Vladimir Putin invaded Ukraine, remember the story?"

"Yes."

"Putin and Xi Jinping, the leader of China had a pact, concerning the time of the Olympics when the Chinese were the host. I think we are looking for a Ukrainian."

"But you thought at the beginning the problem was something to do with COVID and China, but now it's the Madame Juliet and you think it's a problem from Ukraine. I do not see why the French, who were trying to come to a diplomatic solution with the Russians, Macron tried his best, should be a target. We should probably expect an attack on Russia next," says Brendan.

"The point is, we do not have any idea if the problem is a person or persons or Russia and Ukraine or China and COVID and whether everything was put in place before our departure with a timetable to gradually destroy us, or if it's new since our departure and this seems very unlikely as it will be suicide."

"Kamikaze," said Henri.

"-神風maybe," said Abe, "maybe but I hope not."

BERT (best ever robot thing), 史上最高のロボットの事best robot of all time.

BERT robots have been produced in Japan. They are similar to Ruperts but do not look human, not at all. They have a large head, 450 millimetres in diameter with a face like emogee or anime in white with black eyes 75 mm and a blue torso, 300mm in diameter that remains on a white ball of 450 mm, diameter. There are six appendages that appear and retract at random as they scoot about on the ball. The eyes change colour or become screens with information. Also, they blink, which is charming and disarming at the same time.

On occasion, when extreme leverage is necessary, two appendages form a triangle with the ball for increased stability. The BERTs look like a 2-metre-high dumbbell until the appendages appear; then they are a little scary. The appendages resemble tentacles with hands. There are reports of them moving about at high speed, horizontally with the ball and head both spinning and with their appendages shaking around. In this case, they are very scary, but comically so.

They communicate only in Japanese and English but understand all languages and of course, there is their own language of robots. They are controlled by Abe Ito and his team. There are a hundred of them on every spaceship. They take care of maintenance, cleaning, and in case of emergency as first response triage with their nanotechnology and nanorobots that they send from their body and as marshals and guides. Their tasks are very limited but their capacity is enormous. The small nanorobots that swarm on the problem are also a little scary.

The instructions to people appear on their eyes and on the back of their heads. For example, 「私に従ってください」 'suivez moi.' Follow me. This message is always accompanied by a bow.

Independence, 16 February

After the emergency conference, the teams were set up as follows.

The BERTs will monitor all the actions of all robots 24/7.

Brendan's team with Ludovic Schmidt and his team will investigate all the archives and personnel files of all the people on board all the spaceships. People from each country will be identified as appropriate for investigation in each vessel.

Rene Suchet, Brad Smith, and Gabriella will work with Mike Prentis's scanner team to check all the components of the spacecraft with plans and specifications as built to search for anomalies. It is a monumental task.

Meeka decides to hunt more robots.

March 2

"You are looking very lemon this morning," said Gabriella, skates, coffee as usual.

"Agreed, how is the scanner team going?"

"We have discovered that not all the information on the registration dockets is accurate," says Gabriella.

"How much?" Henri says.

"Lots," said Gabriella, "some components of the wheels have different numbers, the nacelles ditto."

"So, do you think this is a substitution or falsification of records or sabotage?"

"It's difficult, but if it is sabotage, then the mission is in grave danger," says Gabriella.

"Continue with Russia, wheels and nacelles and then Australia, this will also be the same for South Africa and South America. First priority please, Gabriella," said Henri.

Gabriella skates away; Henri makes the equivalent of a frown. If the nacelles and wheels fail, the mission is dead. The light-speed propulsion is Henri's number 1 priority.

Meeka is not concerned as Henry had reassured him, so goes off to chase more BERTS.

2 April 10.00 a.m., onboard spaceship Arc Royal 6 (no 1)

The captain is Commander Aubry Elliott, 1.75 metres tall, skinny with ginger hair and green eyes. He speaks with a Lancashire accent.

"We can anticipate our visit by the scanner team tomorrow Mike," says Aubry, "maybe we should check our systems to decouple, 1 and 2, check the airlocks and so on."

"Or maybe not," said Mike, "we don't want to tempt fate."

"I think I will run an automatic check, it will take about 30 minutes and if we get all green, then, all good, if not, we stop the systems check, okay?"

"Yep, if ok we can run the full six-hour test."

2 April Earth, Palma Systems Pasedena Inc. (PSPI) 09.00 hours

Palma Systems are subcontractors to nacelle manufacturers, **Northrop Grumman Corporation.** Now closed as the fleet had gone but this morning there was an emergency meeting of the scientists who had developed the nanotechnology which self-repairs welds and fractures on the spacecraft. It was a triumph of technology and would, if it had not been top secret, it would have been a very commercially successful product. They were in their favourite café, a corner spot by the window overlooking the square. A table had been made up for them, actually, just two placed together with a cheerful red and check tablecloth. Croissants and preserves, water and their favourite Italian coffee were laid out.

The technology consists of a liquid skin that is sprayed on the metal and once activated, which happens automatically after a couple of hours, would repair the damage and then effectively go back to sleep.

An excellent and foolproof product but while relocating some old panels to another warehouse, it was discovered that some panels had been eaten by the nanons. Hence the meeting.

"It is a disaster," says Max, head of the nine scientists and technicians that developed the product. "The technology can be reversed by a close proximity frequency signal in the infrared range but now the spaceships are gone," he pauses to let that problem hang there, "it seems impossible to fix. The welds could just start to melt like butter on a nano slice of toast."

"Very funny," said Terrence, second-in-command of the nine, "but what can we do?"

"Nothing," said Max, "except call Madam President and that won't be a comfortable call."

Max and the other five leave but Aleksander, Kostyantyn and Fedir all stay. All Ukrainian and Fedir, the only woman and the most militant after the Russian invasion of Ukraine on 24 February 2022. She lost her complete family in Putin's war.

"I think we got away with it," Fedir said, "They don't know about the self-destruction, programme, just the nano problem."

"And they don't know the reason for our action," says Aleksander, who lost his entire family to Chinese COVID.

"Well, they have had their first Merry Christmas from us," said Kostyantyn, "and more to come," said Aleksander.

They finished their coffee and left.

White House, 2 April 09.30 Hours

"Madame President, we have a problem," said Gerald who had entered the office with his usual calm manner, except, this morning, he did not look at all calm.

"What is it?" Marika said, with coffee in hand.

"I received a call from PSPI, subcontractors of Northrup Grummon under NASA."

"And?"

"And, the nano skin can reverse and eat the metal."

"You're kidding!"

"No, this is very serious."

"Can we contact the mission?"

"Well, I don't know, the world leaders decided that after the departure in April 2043, it would be better to cut all ties because neither could then help the other and finally, there would be no one on Earth."

"They are travelling at 400,000 mph which is 111 miles per second. They are now 3,504,000,000, miles from us. It will take 5.23 hours to contact them, after and if we can run the dishes again."

"Get on it immediately, Gerald, please."

Gerald closed the door. Marika, looking prematurely grey, sank into the chair and began to cry and not for the first time.

Gerald picks up his phone.

On board Boomerang 14.50 Hours

"Well, you're all clear, scans complete, no problems," says Mike Prentis.

"Thank you, Mike," says Chloe Johnson, Captain of Boomerang, "it's a relief."

"No problem," says Mike in a poor Australian accent. "Where next?"

"The Poms," said Mike in another poor accent, this time English.

15.30 hours, the first sign of corruption of the nano skin on nacelle number 40.

2 April 15.00 hours, onboard space Arc Royal 6 (no 1)

"Good day, Aubry, we're a little bit late, maybe we could set up the robots?" Mike says.

"Good idea, coffee?"

"Yes."

"Of course," said Gabriella.

"How did it go with the Australians?" Aubry says.

"Very good, full scan, no problems but we need to establish a series of cameras to monitor everything," says Mike.

"And it's a huge task," said Gabriella, sipping her coffee and spinning on her skates, a new trick.

"Do you have any more information about the situation?" Aubry said.

"Nothing, we know the explosion on the Chinese Lie-Long was sabotage but we do not know if the explosion on board the French Madame Juliet was also. Of the two, we are more worried about the French situation."

The configuration of the two spaceships, Arc Royal 6 and Arc Royal 6(1) is back to back. There are four wheels and 16 nacelles. As a result, one faces the front and on another occasion, it faces the rear. A rotation of 180 degrees each month solves this problem without the need to decouple and risk an airlock problem. The fleet formation also changes every month so there is a different ship at the head of the conical formation.

This month, Arc Royal 6(1) is in the lead.

Gabriella reflects on how elegant the fleet appeared, scorching through space, each ship with its signature colour. There is no sense of the passage of time here; the only imperative is to write the story.

2 April 15.00 hours, onboard spaceship Zulu

The formation of the fleet looks like a cone.

The lead ship is five miles ahead of the next two, which are five miles ahead of the next three which are five miles ahead of the last three. In plan, the two have a two-mile vertical separation; the three miles and the last three are five miles, like aeroplanes on VFR (flight rules).

In the last row of three are Zulu, USS Independence, and Le Belle Foret, from South Africa. Next are Boomerang, Madame Juliet and China's Lie-Long, next are Vostov 4 and Voyager 1-6 at the front is Arc Royal 6(1).

The Zulu Bridge is huge. The same as Boomerang and the Belle Foret and with the best view of the entire fleet.

Zulu's co-captain is Mlungisi Manqoba which in Afrikaans is 'die een wat orde bring, die een wat in hopelose situasies oorw`in,' the one who brings order, the one who overcomes in hopeless situations.

His name describes him perfectly.

He is very tall at two metres and very proud. There are two teams on the bridge; the other is headed by co-pilot Sebastian Ritter, a German short with blond hair.

"It's the best place," Sebastian said.

"Yes," says Mlungisi, "a little far to see the scanning team in operation on Arc Royal 6 with the naked eye, all those little robots scampering about, very comical."

"It's only 15 miles, put it on the screen," says Abebe.

White House 16. 00 Hours

"The message was late to go, the technological problems were really tricky but, they would get the message by 16.23."

"Thanks, Gerald, I hope it's time."

Royal Arc 6 (1) 16.20 Hours.

"We're ready to go," said Mike.

"I need another coffee," said Gabriella without skates, "two minutes please."

Zulu 16.22 Hours

"**What the F###?**" Mlungisi says. "Debris?" As the screens flash red and sirens sound.

"Emergency manoeuvre DELTA, immediately," said Abebe, "it is not debris it is the Boomerang."

Arc-Royal 6(1) 16.23

"Good to go," said Gabriella.

The emergency line is screaming.

"It is Earth," said Gabriella, a message from the White House, her coffee falling from her hand.

They listen in shock.

"Stop the scans immediately," Gabriella shouted.

Boomerang 16. 23.15sec

"All ships, this is Boomerang code red, we have just suffered a catastrophic disintegration, minutes ago. We require emergency assistance please, the ship is ruptured, and falling apart, there are bodies everywhere," says Chloe Johnson. "We are deploying the escape emergency pods."

From the bridge of Zulu, it was possible to see the scene of destruction unfold. There were no explosions, parts of windows remain but the walls have simply disappeared, the glass of the staircase balustrade remains but the ceilings and walkways are all gone, seats are floating around, glass table tops with no legs, people with glasses just have the lenses floating before their face as the metal hinges melt. It is a surreal situation but as floors and walls gradually disappear and the spaceship is de-pressurised, people explode.

The robots, the BERTS fly around with follow-me messages on their screens. Many people had time to put on spacesuits and many also managed to get to the pods but about 1,800 of the 4,000 died. It is a total catastrophe.

Chloe talks to the whole fleet.

"This is Chloe, Captain of Boomerang, well, I was, I am on board shuttle number BM53, I think that around 2,200 of us remain, more or maybe less, we will remain in space for the moment in case of contamination to other ships but what could be done is to salvage the spares and stores and equipment, anything metal-free which may be useful later. I suggest at a point three miles to starboard. We will be able to dedicate the robots to coordinate retrieval and catalogue everything later. We have few wounded; we are either dead and now part of space or alive. Chloe out."

Arc Royal 6(1) 16. 7 p.m.

The emergency stop was a success; the robots were all assembled on wheel 1 to start the infrared scans but were programmed to start at 16.30 hours. A small miracle, thank your White House.

"We will establish the coordinates exactly for storage and hook up by globe link at 17.00 hours with the heads of other ships," says Henri.

"Whatever," said Gabriella.

17.00 hours

All the chiefs were on the globes and the screens were running in all the ships including the shuttles and evacuation pods. Gabriella with coffee, Ludo with tea and Henri with an air of solemnity.

"Welcome, everyone, I won't say good evening because it's not," said Henri. "This is our first real crisis. Perhaps we have been lucky so far away, that has passed, and this is serious. We have sent word back to Earth."

Difficult Choices, 12 September USS Independence 10.00 Hours.

It took five months and ten days to recover from the disaster. All non-metallic and useful parts, stores and components were placed in a large wheel of 300-meter diameter built from the non-metal tubes of the wreck, with a nylon rope net covering the space in the middle; it looks like a big tyre. There are huge Michelin men painted on the sides at 30-metre intervals. BERTS, no doubt!

The survivors were dispersed to the other ships, 600 on Arc Royal 6 and 400 on Arc Royal 6 (1), 650 on USS Independence, 100 on USS Voyager (3), 250 on Vostov 4 and 200 on Lie-Long.

All have adapted well and some say it's like a vacation.

The infrared problem remains as it is present by nature in the spectrum of light from the sun which emits more than half its energy in the infrared field. As a result, over time, all spacecraft will become susceptible to this and fall apart.

Meanwhile, the sabotage of Lie-Long is unexplained and remains a huge problem.

As head of the mission, Henry had to decide what to do. He convened a conference globe for all ships in the mission.

"Hello all, two things, it's time to decide what to do and I can report progress on the light propulsion system. This is where we are."

"Go for it," said Gabriella, with coffee, skates, and a laugh, which she didn't feel was justified.

"Okay, first the good news, I finished the light propulsion system."

Thunderous applause, Henri bowed and shone lemon.

"But there are not enough minerals here to build a system that would operate a spaceship, only a shuttle, and this is a further huge problem."

"How does it work?" Gabriella said already knowing the answer.

"It bends the space by projecting a beam of particles, which we then cross."

"And so," said Gabriella, feeding him another line.

"So, I have to go back to Earth."

"And," said Gabriella.

"And...Find the minerals, build sufficient systems for all the ships and get back here."

"And," said Gabriella, feeding him another line.

"Six months, possibly one year and without guarantee of success."

"What are the possibilities that you will not be back?" Stephanie Miller, Captain of USS Voyager 09 says expressing everyone's thoughts.

"60/40, maybe 70/30 at best with all systems, but a 95% mission failure if I come back without them."

There was total silence. Ludo broke it.

"And the degradation of the ships because of the infrared."

"I calculate 5–8 years, no more."

"It's clear," said Abe Ito, "there is no choice, you have to go back and I think I'll go with you."

"And we on Zulu?" Abebe said, captain of the Zulu, pausing for effect. "We have decided to return to planet Earth. If others wish to go with us, we can take 500."

Total silence again. Chloe broke it this time.

"And you will need a pilot," said Chloe, "and it seems that I am free."

"But why go now?" Aubry said. "why not wait for Henry's return?"

116

"Because we have time to go back but maybe, we do not have time to move forward."

"We understand your position," says Henri, "as of now, the mission in its present form is finished. We have slim choices but we have them and we must take them. It's all a risk but we have another objective in going back and that is to develop a solar reflective paint that can be applied to the remaining ships. If we can do that, the mission will still be possible."

"How long before you leave?" Gabriella says.

"Three days, we must transfer the device to the big (30-person shuttle), run some tests and, then, we go. We will also take two of our precious Ruperts and two BERTS. Seven of us in total, it is a lucky number."

"Amen to that," said Gabriella. "I will send word to the White House."

15 September the Shuttle number USS 1101, 0830 hours, at the last moment, General Fletcher, known as 'Leroy' by his friends, decided to join the team. Eight is also a lucky number in Chinese and Lie-Long needs some luck.

The nose of the shuttle now looked like a porpoise, smooth and grey around three metres long but with 6 tubes of 2 metres × 300 mm diameter protruding from the nose, not porpoise-looking at all. The tubes focus on the beam of particles that distorts the space.

A message already sent to the White House read 'Arrival 15 September at 1400 hours, urgent meetings to organise with the jet propulsion laboratory in Pasadena, with Du Pont' and 'MP materials', owners of the 'Mountain Pass mine'…**And IRIS must be there.**

Henri had used 95% of the store he had on board the mission of Europium in the building of the light propulsion system. Europium is atomic number 63. It has a half-life of 8,593 years. It is found in the Kolu peninsular, Bayan Obo in Mongolia and the 'Mountain Pass Rare Earth Mine' in California. It is one of the rarest minerals and is used mainly in small quantities in optoelectronic devices. Henri needs about 130 tons plus some spare.

World production per year is 100 tons. It must be protected from the effects of moisture or oxygen by storage under an inert liquid.

The interior of the shuttle is very large, a small gally, WC and 30 seats, adjustable and able to recline, upholstered in a grey material with automatic harnesses. The interior is illuminated by the walls that glow with soft luminescence seats, those not used in the flight, collapse into the floor making a larger storage space. There are three pilot seats each fully equipped with all the necessary controls plus the 3D screens.

All flight information is displayed on the screens.

The star map indicates the position of the shuttle and the destination displayed with a colour that indicates the fuel expenditure from yellow, good, to black empty. F. 9 8 7 6 5 4 3 2 1 E.

Planet Earth is indicated by a checkered flag. One of Henri's little jokes.

The sun is indicated as the point at which the shuttle must disengage the light drive, or spin off into space. It's a nice round number 500 seconds (8.33r) minutes.

"Have a good trip and good luck," said Ludo on behalf of us all. All the lights on all spaceships turn green as the shuttle breaks into formation and starts a huge left turn of 180 degrees.

08.35

"We have fuel, chewing gum and we are wearing sunglasses," Charlotte says in a terrible parody of the Blues Brothers.

"Let's go."

Charlotte carries out the pre-flight check and Henri inputs the coordinates. All of them are indicated on the 3D display.

"Let's check three times," says Abe Ito, "just in case."

"All good, Abe, here we go."

Charlotte removes the cover of the switch. It plays a Micky Mouse Luny Tunes jingle, another of Henri's little jokes.

"This may not work," said Henri.

"Turn the switch," says Abe.

The soft backlight of the interior dims and changes to red, the human eye can see dark objects better in the red spectrum. Charlotte turns the switch to the right. A pause then a very strange feeling.

In 3D, the shuttle appears as a small rhombus with a smiley face emogee and the number 8 flashing green. A line joins the rhombus with hundreds of small dots with more numbers and planet Earth is illuminated blue. The sun is yellow and has the critical countdown numbers for disengagement. It also has an emogee of two hands clasped as if in prayer. BERT's again 5.30. 59 in mili seconds, in real-time 58.57,56 etc. 5.29.59 etc.

On Henri's right screen, the position of the navigator, the nose of the shuttle, appears like a video game, a tube full of stars and six laser lines in red, pointing to one star after another at a disconcerting speed. Next to the tube, just darkness.

"Coffee anyone?" Rupert said.

"I'll get it," said Leroy.

They seem like a comic duo, Leroy, short, plump 1.75 metre, with blue hair and Rupert, 2 metres tall, all in purple with his big head. He resembles a lollipop held by an 'Umpa Lumpa' from 'Charlie and the Chocolate Factory'.

Leroy puts the coffees carefully on the tray, takes some biscuits and napkins and performs a small bow as he presents the coffees, like an aeroplane hostess.

"You look very attractive, I mean, Fletching, like a hostess," says Charlotte with a smile, which, being very tall was on a level with Leroy when she sat.

"It's nothing, Charlotte, do you think my nails conflict with this outfit?"

"Not at all, Leroy, you look adorable."

Every now and then, there was a small change of direction, the line on the screen to the right of Henri moved. The fuel numbers continue their steady countdown.

"I was thinking, what will happen if we hit something at the speed of light," says Charlotte, turning her long neck to Henri.

Henri shrugs his shoulders and smiles and leans over at BERTs 1 and 2.

"Don't worry, BERTs, it's all under control."

The two BERTs start rolling on the floor while their screens are displaying...Follow me.

"They're outrageous," said Abe, "you can't control them."

"They are new," said Henri, "but I will have a word."

Henri bows to them in Japanese fashion and they roll away and sit on the ceiling.

Abe Ito smiled.

9.8 On fuel numbers, 4.30 hours on the clock.

"So far so good," said Charlotte, looking more confident than she felt.

Ruperts 1 and 2 had turned their chairs around and inclined them so as to trap the BERTS, (who were both once again on the deck), with their feet. In protest, they spun their globes in an irritated manner. A parody of a child's hissy fit.

The Ruperts continued to chat in Japanese, which Abe listened to with a smile but also for a while, with an eyebrow raised. Maybe he will talk with Henry about it.

The next two hours pass without incident, Leroy supplied coffee and Charlotte supplied a comment on the progress made, but in fact, there is nothing to do, no corrections, all is automatic. But Henri is troubled, at 2 hours 45 minutes, the distance should be the midpoint, but it was short by 3 minutes at the speed of light or, 33,480,000 miles. As a result, another 74.4 minutes would be added and for which, there is insufficient fuel.

"We need to talk," says Henri, smiling at Charlotte, Leroy and Abe and we must disable the BERTS and Ruperts.

Leroy jumped out of his seat and amusingly, was still the same height, approximately. He goes over to the Roberts.

"Hello, boys," said Leroy, putting on his general's voice, "it's time for a nap."

The BERTS perform a quick rotation of their globes and the Ruperts just smile and close their eyes.

"We have a problem," said Abe and Henri at the same time.

Charlotte raised an eyebrow and Leroy put his hands over her ears. "Perhaps you should not hear this."

"Really, Fletch," she said with a wicked smile, "I'm a big girl."

"You first," said Abe, looking at Henri.

"Thing is, as you know, we must cut the light propulsion drive by the time we reach the sun and then within that 93,000,000 miles to Earth, decelerate from 186,000 mps to 17,500 mph by the Karman line (100 km or 62 miles) at which point we enter the Earth's atmosphere with heat shield deployed and touch down in Burbank, or if we miss it, we burn up in the atmosphere or we jump out into space."

"Do we have a choice in any of these scenarios?" Leroy said having abandoned his general's accent.

"No, but I think we are not getting the correct information," said Henri.

"Are you sure?" Charlotte said.

"I checked everything and I am unable to make a mistake, it is not possible."

"And so?" Abe said, looking inquisitive.

"And so," said Henri, "it's the robots and my guess, it's the BERTS."

"Damn!" said Charlotte, "little beggars."

"I had been listening to their conversation," said Abe, "they were talking about the big joke."

"What?" Henry said.

"The BERTS," said Abe, "were talking about it."

"Activate them," says Henry.

The BERTS come to attention, their screens say good day and they bow on their globes. A neat trick.

"Explain," says Henri.

"What?" BERT 2 said.

"You know."

"We were studying other languages to see if the meanings were the same, for example, the words, humour, and riddle, good joke and bad joke because bad also seems to mean good, you see the problem and so we devised a little plan to test human intelligence as opposed to robots intelligence."

"And?" Abe says in Japanese.

"Well, robots win because Henri discovered the anomaly and Henri is a robot, right?"

"Okay, good test, can you put the clock and fuel readings back to their correct readings?"

"Of course, it's done."

"And can you do it without moving?"

"Of course, maybe you want another test?"

"No, you're ok," said Charlotte, Henri, Abe and Leroy with one voice.

Everyone laughs and the BERTS pivot on their globes. Their screens say 'Good Joke'.

"Coffee, anyone?" Leroy says.

1 E (empty)

93,000,000 miles to planet Earth, the light drive stops automatically, with no small amount of apprehension felt by Henri, Charlotte, Leroy and Abe. Heat shields deployed rapidly decreasing speed. BERTS are displaying 'all good, thank you BERT'

"Burbank-Glendale Pasadena control, (always in English) this is shuttle number USS 1101 'de profond espace' deep space, USS Independence we are 2 minutes out at 450 knots and slowing, requesting landing instructions," says Charlotte.

Crackling on the line...

13.59 hours

"Burbank control, this is USS shuttle 1101..."

"USS Shuttle 1101, you are clear to land on runway 15/33. Wind is 5 mph west."

"Thank you, Burbank."

-280 knots, full flaps, parachute drogues, 150 knots at 130 ft., 90 knots, 100, at 50ft, 30ft, and 10ft and down, full retro and stop. The nose dips on the double-nose wheel.

"Welcome back, please taxi to Gate 9 and hold. We will come for you."

It was a strange sight for a domestic airport, the shuttle with its badge of return, a blackened appearance outside and also with the three parachutes drogues still attached and flapping around.

"Well played, Henri," said Charlotte.

"Job to do, BERTs," said Fletch in his serious voice.

The BERTS spin and their screens say 'Follow me' as they fly to the ground, and surprise everyone as they stand to attention on both sides of the ramp.

The Unexpected Encounter.
11.00 a.m., September 16th NASA Conference Room 9a

"Welcome, Madame President, Henri, Abe, Charlotte and General Fletcher. How can I help you?" Vincent le Grange 11 said.

"Well, what have you done with my legacy?" Leroy said with a smile.

Vincent le Grange11 was now head of NASA, short and black with green eyes and the same colour hair.

"Following your tradition," said V, with an even bigger smile, everyone laughed, but it's a little quiet here at the moment.

"We could change all that," said Henri. "We need your old shuttles, all 3 remaining and functioning."

There had been 135 flight missions from 1981–2011; this next will be number 136.

"Don't worry about launching it, we will build new propulsion systems but we will need three pilots and three co-pilots and we need a capacity payload of 50 tons each."

"That all?" Vincent said with a look of mock astonishment.

"Almost," said Henri, "we also need to build the light-speed drives for the fleet that remains, seven of them and they need more space than the shuttle capacity, so that's a problem."

"Is that all?"

"Almost," said Henri, "we also need to build some ships for basic cargo and send them to the space station where they will be loaded with the light drive."

"Is That All Yet?" Vincent Said.

"Almost," said Henri with a bow, "we need to redesign the navigation systems for the shuttles and we need to send 130 tons of raw Europium, which we don't yet have of course, to the space station for loading in the shuttles, so I can get this extra weight into Earth orbit."

"Is that all?" Marika said picking up on the humour.

"Almost," said Henri, "we have to find out how and by whom the sabotage of the Chinese spacecraft was carried out," said Henri with a raise of his eyebrow.

"And?" Abe said, feeding the line to Henri.

"And, we need hardware to stop the spacecraft from dissolving in infrared."

"That's all?" IRIS said.

"No, almost," said Henri, "do you have some coffee for the humans?" He said with a sweeping gesture to the whole assembly.

"It's a big list," says Vincent.

"Thank you," said Henri, missing the point exactly. Everyone else laughed.

"May take some time," says Vincent.

"No problem," says Henri, "is six months enough?"

"Yes, but not sure about the painting. Don't think our old ladders will work."

11.00 a.m., September 17th NASA Conference Room 9a

Henri, Iris, Gerald, Marika, Abe, Leroy (Fletch) and the Rupert robots and the two BERTS, were all there. Charlotte went to Australia to see her parents.

Yesterday's tasks were set up, reunions with Dupont for painting and MP materials for Europium. The sabotage problem is far more difficult.

"Abe, Henri, Leroy and I were talking," said IRIS, and we came to a conclusion.

"Which is?" Marika said.

"The sabotage must have taken place here when the nacelles were manufactured and we want to discuss this under the cover of the new items to be manufactured under licence by the full team of **Palma Systems Pasedena Inc. (PSPI)."**

"We want the lot of them at the meeting, no exceptions and we want the lot here today," said IRIS, "and we **will get to the bottom of things."**

"They will not suspect anything but will reveal the truth to us. The meeting will be with all of them and Henri, Rupert, BERT 1, Abe, Leroy, Vincent and me," says IRIS.

"You know, IRIS, you can be a tad frightening sometimes," said Henri, with a blink of his robotic eye, which had two little grim reaper emogees displayed on them.

"Nice touch, Henri," said IRIS.

Meeting 14.00 Hours, 17 September NASA Conference Room 9a

"Welcome," said Henri, "I am the Chief of the Space Mission. I am, as you can see, a robot. We came back to Earth because we needed to solve certain problems. You will have heard about that. You are here because you were part of the manufacturing team. Thank you for your previous service and for coming here a short notice. We hope that you will help us again."

Henry bowed.

"Please sit down, I will make the introductions. On my right, General Fletcher, you will know him, then, Vincent the new head of NASA, then Abe Ito of the 'green eyes' and the robots Rupert and BERT 1 and IRIS who are the same as me. Coffee, water, tea?"

"We have specifications for components, we hoped, Max and Terrence that the whole original 9 team would be able to assist."

Fletcher chips in, "Where are Aleksander, Kostyantyn and Fedir?"

"I called them and invited them here, but it seems that they have now disappeared," said Max, with an air of embarrassment.

"Okay," says IRIS, "no problem, please, study the specifications and respond to us by next week. Details and submission requirements are in your briefing package."

"Do you have any questions?" Vincent said.

Max was a little worried, it would be an immediate instruction to proceed, but without the full team, it might be more than a little difficult.

"No, thank you for the invitation, you will have our offer next week," says Max.

They leave and head to their café.

"Find them," says Henri, "shut the airports, post bulletins at all the ports, get every agency on the case and make them come."

"It is in hand," says IRIS, "what was in the documents?"

"Nothing really," said Henri, "just a request for their hourly rate and some redundant components."

"They will smell a rat," said Vincent.

"Exactly," said Henri.

"Max was speaking the truth," said IRIS, "I read his mind. He thinks they did something but he didn't know what."

"Good, but we do," said Henri. "We must find them."

LAX 14.30 Hours

Alexsander had prepared his disguise and fake passport just after the departure of the mission in April 2043, Kostantyn was going to Europe and Fedir to Mexico, or so she says.

Last call for flight Avianca 429 in Rio.

"Flight 429, hold on runway 7L/25R."

14.52 hours

"Flight AVA 429 heavy to Rio, you are cleared for take-off on runway 7L/25R, please climb to flight level 2.5 and await further instructions. Out."

"LAX, this is flight 429 will climb right to flight level 2.5 and await further instruction. Out."

Flight 429

"Ladies and gentlemen, this is your captain, welcome aboard flight 429 to Rio. It's a long flight of 18 hours 25 minutes so please relax; we will serve drinks after we clear the turbulence. Please stay seated and keep your seat belts on."

Aleksandra, now Jens Mickelson, relaxed, he was off and free.

Residence Inn Los Angeles (3.7 miles from the Jet Propulsion Lab) 18.35 Hours

Everyone was back in their suites, though Marika and Gerald who were back in Washington, and promising to meet every month.

"Henri? It's LAPD, Sergeant Marquez. We searched Aleksander's house, he was in a hurry but we hacked his computer and found a ticket for a Jens Mickelson, for Rio but the plane took off at 14.52 hours."

"Are you sure it's him?" Henri said.

"More or less, we matched his fingerprints. We can pick him up in Bogota."

"Excellent, good work, any news of the other two?"

"Not yet."

"Please contact Bogotá and ask them to detain him. We will fly to Bogota on the next flight. Thank you very much, Sergeant Marquez," said Henri.

"No problem," said Marquez.

20.00 Bogotá Air Traffic Control

"Flight AVA 429 from Los Angeles, we have you on approach runway 13L/31R, please be advised we have an international arrest warrant for one of your passengers, Jens Mickelson on a Norwegian passport. Please ensure he is the last to leave and is accompanied by your stewards to the arrivals lounge where he will be arrested."

Flight 429

"Ladies and gentlemen, we will soon arrive in Bogota. Please put your seats in an upright position and straighten and fasten your seat belts. Our stewards will pick up your landing passes."

20.07 hours

"Ladies and gentlemen, thank you for flying with Avianca, welcome to Bogotá, please make sure you have all your belongings with you."

20.10 hours

"Mr Mickelson? There is an emergency message for you, could you please accompany me to the arrivals building? Please let everyone else go first, thank you, sir."

Jens heads towards the arrivals escorted by two attendants. He is a little worried.

"Good afternoon, Mr Mickelson," said a guard carrying a pistol and wearing sunglasses.

Now he is worried.

"Sit down, sir, please. We have an international arrest warrant against you from the United States. Miguel will escort you to the detention centre where you will be detained until the arrival of the American agents. Would you like coffee or water?"

Aleksander put his face in his hands. One way or another, he must call the others.

They had organised a method to contact in case of emergency, a message (cat **bag bag cat**) would be put in the *Los Angeles Daily News*, personal column.

"Can I make a phone call?"

"Sure, how's your coffee?" Miguel said.

Aleksander (Mickelson) was wondering if the pistol worked, guns surely didn't work anymore, but it was disconcerting nonetheless.

18 September

Kostyantyn took his newspapers to the café as usual. He asks for a black coffee with a glass of water and a Danish pastry. He took his usual seat and opened the newspaper. A quick look at the ads, he sees **'cat bag bag cat.'** He swallows his coffee and runs home.

Fedir decided not to go to the meeting at the space lab as requested in Terrence's text message, but to take a vacation. She was at home at 7.45 o'clock when the doorbell rang.

"Mademoiselle Fedir? Delivery for you. You need to sign."

"OK, I'll come down."

She opened the door, and gasped, four NYPD policemen were on the porch.

"Hands behind your back, you are under arrest."

Two policemen took Fedir to the car, two went up to the apartment. The forensic team arrived after six minutes.

Kostyantyn had two identities, one as a professor of 'Palma Systems' where he looks like an athlete, with a bald head and very muscular, the other has his home in San Francisco, 347 miles, a short flight, where he spends his weekends as a member of the gay community, always wearing a wig of blue, or orange and always with his nails painted.

The warning announcement by the personal chronicle worked perfectly. It took a simple code to place it automatically. Thank you Aleksander whose prefix **A**, this warning was.

21 September Room Nos. 8 and 9

Fedir and Aleksander are now in NASA custody. They are in different locations.

The room is big and not intimidating, there is food and drinks. It is very civilised. There is a guard at the door. Henri and IRIS are present with FEDIR.

Room 8

"Fedir, do you know why are you here?" IRIS said.

"No idea," says Fedir.

"Do you know about the space mission?"

"Of course, I worked on it."

"Do you know Aleksander?" IRIS said.

"Of course, we are colleagues."

"Where is he?"

"No idea."

"He's here," said Henri.

Fedir seemed a little worried and she was very nervous at being studied by robots. She takes a glass of water.

"We will be back," says Henri.

They leave.

Room 9

Aleksander, appearing very relaxed, was drinking his coffee. The room is comfortable with sofas, books, table and chairs with drinks and breakfast. There is a big TV on one wall. Leroy (General Fletcher), Abe and a Rupert enters the room. They make a bizarre view, short Leroy with blue hair, Abe Ito very tall with samurai green hair and eyes and a Robot.

"Hello Alexsander," Abe said with a polite bow.

Abe, taking his coffee and one of the chairs, Leroy and Rupert remain standing.

"Why did you change your name?" Rupert said smiling at him.

Aleksander thinks about that.

"No comment."

"Why did you sabotage the components?" Rupert said.

"No comments," says Alexsander.

"Why did Kostantyn sabotage the components?" Rupert said.

"No comment."

"Do you realise why Rupert is here?" Abe said.

Aleksander feels a chill in his spinal column.

Rupert, Abe and Fletch all leave the room.

Conference A

Abe, Henri, Rupert 1, Leroy, and IRIS are all assembled in the conference room.

"Let them stew," said Henri, "the problem is that although we may listen to their thoughts, they do not know where Kostyantyn is."

"Also," said Abe, "neither knew how the sabotage was accomplished. They only worked on the components. We know what the components are but we do not know how they interact with each other and we do not know the time or the trigger. We must find Kostantyn."

"We will have another go tonight, then, move them to the police station and keep them in custody for 48 hours, then charge them with sabotage," says IRIS.

18.00 hrs conference A

Abe, Henri, Leroy, Rupert 1 and IRIS were all sitting around the table. Fedir and Alexsander are escorted by two guards. They are surprised to be together.

"So, you didn't have Kostantyn," Fedir said with a laugh.

"You are right," said IRIS, "but we also know that you do not know and that worries you."

"How do you know that?" Fedir says.

"Because," said IRIS, "I can read your thoughts."

Fedir laughs.

"Perhaps, there is some information in your sub-conscience," says IRIS.

"Find it then," said Fedir with a smile.

Aleksander doesn't smile.

"The problem for you," says Leroy, "is that if she does, you will become a vegetable." He smiled back at Fedir.

"Tell them, Fedir," says Aleksander.

"What?"

"About San Francisco."

"There you go," said IRIS, "not difficult, was it?"

IRIS, Rupert 1, Henri, Abe and Leroy all leave the room. Fedir and Aleksander seem stunned.

"Shame," said IRIS, "Fedir would have made a good carrot."

"Or tomato," said Abe with a laugh.

"Let's go," said Henri, "lots more to do."

Kostyantyn

The smartest of the three, IQ 135, the architect of sabotage, had developed the mechanism that would activate the destructor programme by adapting the materials to self-destruct at predetermined times, whether in use or in store.

He had also developed components specifically for the Chinese and Russian spaceships, in secret, of which Aleksander and Fedir are not aware. He had also programmed some random events. He was psychotic. Brilliant, and totally crazy.

But, he had a doubt, would Aleksander or Fedir reveal his San Francisco connection? He needed another identity.

22 September Zulu 18.50 hours

The return trip was going well, no problem, morale is good, it is a happy place.

Abebe was asleep when the emergency signal sounded.

It took five minutes to arrive at the bridge; Abebe was there in two.

"What is the problem?" He said calmly.

Amahle (the beautiful one) is second-in-command.

"Storage room in wheel 4 starboard side, a fire."

The fire was soon extinguished, automatically, robots were on the scene.

"They report the problem is with a wiring loom in a machine case."

Amahle frowns. "And there is a message, **have a nice day;** it's burnt into the casing," says Amahle.

"Still a year away from Earth, we might not make it, send an urgent message to NASA," said Abebe.

23 September NASA, 00.22 hrs

The lines are monitored 24/7 by the commander of the 'Henri' watch. Nickname for the hot news line.

Jimmy Emmerson was duty sergeant. He was new to the job and liked it. He got the message through to Henri PDQ running all the way. He should have just picked up the phone. *Muppet,* he thought.

"Henri?" He panted, out of breath.

"Yes, what is it? Take a breath."

"An emergency message from Zulu, Captain Abebe," he said. "We are still a year away and we just had a fire and there was a message. 'Have a nice day.' Maybe there will be other incidents, maybe we won't get back."

"Send a message to Zulu. We have identified two of the saboteurs and we have them in custody, one is missing but we will find him and he **will talk**. Remain vigilant. Talk soon. Henri out."

The message went, it was optimistic and calming but Henri felt less so.

NASA Conference Room 9a 09.30 hrs 24 September

Henri called everyone together for a brief.

Abe, Leroy, Rupert 1, and IRIS plus LAPD Sergeant Marquez.

"We know that Aleksander and Fedir are not aware of any second identity for Kostantyn and also, they do not know of an address in San Francisco," says Henri.

"It may be a false trail," said Leroy, running his fingers through his blue hair.

"We can trace the names of all LAX departures since September 17th, in fact of all airports on the day," says Sergeant Elena Marquez.

"What if he left by car, then what?" Henri said.

"We can trace his digital footprints but he can always wear gloves. Therefore we must deceive him," says Elena.

"Brilliant," said Abe, "how exactly?"

"By creating a public emergency," Rupert said, "in fact, a national emergency. Play on the fears of the original alien invasion. Something where humanity needs to prove that they are human."

"I like it," said Henri.

"Give me 24 hours," says Rupert 1.

"Brilliant," said Leroy, "meanwhile, Sergeant Marquez, can check all the departures from the airport."

"Let's go," said Henri, "back here tomorrow, at the same time."

The Plan and Fake News

Since the departure of the mission by spaceships and portals, there have been reports of disappearances and people not being quite the same. It was true, but now there were people talking strangely, which was also true because the robots, Ruperts, who could assume whatever form they chose, did so, quite often. The feeling of unease was spreading.

For a month, the media, TV, papers and social media, carried everyday reports of people not being the same.

By the end of October, all world Governments had a program in place for the verification of human identity. It was also becoming, by default, a census and now there were just 1.2 billion people.

For access to services, medical, social, financial, indeed, anything at all, you need a microchip and on the chip is all your information, name, fingerprints, biometric scan and your DNA, what you are and your number. Everyone has a number. Soon, Kostyantyn will appear somewhere.

Paris 1 October

Kostyantyn was very careful and intelligent. He had six complete identities with documents, disguises, housing and money. Here in Paris, he was Pierre Renault, of independent means, and gay. He created this identity six years ago and it was the best. Today he had an appointment with a new friend, Justin at the Eifel Tower for breakfast. The day was clear and bright and it seemed as though everything was perfect, but, a little doubt about the disappearances and controls worried him. What if? He decided he wasn't going to worry about it and walked towards the Eifel Tower, stepped off the pavement and floated in the air.

3 October, the hospital American

"Hello, Mr Renault, how are you?" The doctor said.

Konstantyn thinks about it and sees his leg and arm in plaster and wonders who Konstantyn is.

"You were hit by a car, a broken leg, a broken arm, a cracked rib and a concussion, you were lucky. Rest, you are on a lot of medication."

The doctor telephoned the number in the United States.

5 October

"Hello, Sergeant Marquez? This is the Hospital of America in Paris, Doctor Emmanuel here, I think we have your man."

Henri arranges for Elena Marquez to release Alexsander and Fedir and to transport them to Paris accompanied by Leroy IRIS Rupert1 and Fletch.

6 October, the American hospital.

"Dr Emmanuel? Henri here, we are in reception."

Pavilion 12

"Hello, Mr Renault, how are you this morning?"

"Who is Mr Renault?" Kostyantin says.

"You were, you had a severe concussion. It has passed. In the meantime, you have some visitors."

Aleksander and Fedir enter the room, accompanied by three police. Konstantyn raises an eyebrow.

Kostyantyn thinks Fedir, Kostyantyn thinks Alexsander, Kostyantyn thinks sh***

-IRIS hears their thoughts.

Before their eyes, the fonts change in the IRIS and Henri robots and suddenly the room is no longer a calm place. Elena Marquez stayed, while Rupert and Fletcher took Fedir and Alexsander out in handcuffs. Kostyantin is fixated by the scrolling images in the robot's eyes. He thinks they are terrifying.

"Well," said IRIS, "now you know, or guess, that we can read your thoughts and so, Pierre Renault, or Jens Mickelson, or Jason Gaylord, very funny that one, or Erich Merkle or Simon Smythson, we have you and when you recover enough to travel, you will be back to the United States for a little probing of the mind and after that, if you do not cooperate." She pauses, "You will be a vegetable. Have a good day, Kostyantyn, see you soon."

Kostyantyn thinks the room was a bit scary. When, like an amnesiac, he did not know who he was, he felt comfortable and secure, but now, after the visits, all this has changed.

Now he knows who and what he is and what he is doing.

Now all his identities are known.

Now he is caught and what was the tingle he could feel on the back of his neck, under the skin?

And what is scary really is that the police/robot thing does not speak to him but simply gives him its thoughts.

But distance can be a problem for them. So, one last chance.

He rang the emergency button.

8 October, NASA Conference Room 9A 09.30

"Elena Marquez and Rupert 1, will bring Kostyantyn back here in five days," says Henri and then we will get the information we need.

"The problem remains that we don't know if he will help us," says Abe.

"There's no need to speculate," says Fletcher, "just wait."

"In reality, we are between the rock and the hard place on this one, says IRIS. I can get his thoughts but maybe, because of amnesia, they will not all be there."

"No problem," says Henri. "It will work out. meanwhile, it's time we left for Du Pont. Let's go, we have a flight to catch."

DuPont, 200 Powder Mill Rd. Wilmington FROM 13.00 hours.

The Kapton Polymide was the first material to protect the lenses of the James Webb Space Telescope JWST on 25 December 2021.

Dr Michael Spencer is the head of R&D and was involved in the development of Kapton. IRIS, Henri, Abe and Fletcher were all assembled in conference room 7; it was spacious with a large table with 12 chairs. On an adjacent table, a buffet lunch with sandwiches and drinks. A large screen was on the wall at one end.

"Welcome," said Michael, "please help yourself to refreshments. We have prepared for you a visualisation of our proposal to solve your problem. There are two solutions that are possible. I also invited our team to join us. Let me introduce the team." There were four young people, two women and two men. They spoke in turn, formal and nervous.

"I am Mary Bouchet, technical team leader." Mary was French, with short black hair and very red lips. Very pretty.

"I am Thomas Masters, special effects and computer animation." Thomas was a dual national, Japanese and English, young with very fashionable hair.

"I am Alexandre Jocovic, logistics and planning." IRIS felt a deep anxiety in this young man, Henri and Abe also felt the tension. It was palpable.

"And last but not least, Isabella Calvi," said Micheal. Isabella was unbelievably beautiful and second to the head of R&D. In a normal room, there would be sighs, but this is not a normal room.

"Thomas will take the lead," said Michael.

"You are all familiar with the Webb telescope screen? We think that a similar screen will work too, that is to say, it needs to work until you jump to light-speed. Also, we do not think it will be possible to cloak all surfaces of all vessels. I will run the simulation."

The simulation began with the James Webb shield, then, all the ships appeared, one by one. Boomerang and Zulu are missing. The simulation shows the 5 metre shuttles landing their cargo. The screens are contained in cylinders, hundreds of them each 5 metres high. They are moved by the robots and fixed in position. The simulation then demonstrates waves of radiation approaching from a distant sun; the screens deploy in the direction of the waves, like an umbrella and the waves bounce from umbrella to umbrella and off into space. Each screen on each ship is coordinated to deflect the rays away. Do you have any questions?

"Thank you, Thomas, for your presentation, but yes, many questions," said Abe.

"What if there is 360-degree radiation and how do you decide on the initial placement?"

"Thank you, Abe, we have considered this problem and there is a part 2 presentation which covers that as well. Alexandre, please."

IRIS feels a great nervousness in Alexandre and Abe and Henri exchange glances.

Alexandre was tall and thin with a shock of orange hair. He appeared very cool on the surface.

IRIS detects another spike in anxiety. Alexandre ran part 2.

In this sequence, there is a projected grid, a lattice shape, pointing forward of the ships of about 30 metres in diameter. Each nodal point has a number and upon detection of radiation, the canisters are deployed and fly to specific locations in the grid and from which the screens are then deployed. The screens are powered by their own thrusters and are about 60 × 60 metres when open. The computer will give them three spatial coordinates. At the same time, the spacecraft will change its formation and move into a formation of a cone. Each screen buffers and deflects the rays away to the next and so on. The entire operation will take about three minutes. "It's rather like opening an umbrella," said Mike with a smile.

"And you think this is the best solution?" Abe said.

"It's the best we can do said Alexandre, a computer program is also needed that will interface with all the navigation systems on all the spacecraft."

"It's very complicated," says Abe, "I don't like it, can't you just make some drones?"

"Drones were deployed very successfully in past conflicts, I am sure you're familiar with these and in particular in the Ukraine/Russian war from around 2013 and you know the result of that. Consider this very carefully. It has to be better than your Micky Mouse grids and canisters and lots of bells and whistles."

"Yes, it does appear very complicated, but Palma Systems can sort it."

Another great spike of anxiety is detected by IRIS and Abe and Henri. There is something about Palma Systems then.

"The beauty of this solution is that we only need the canisters to cover the shape of the cone, not the complete surface of all the vessels," said Mike.

"Exactly said Alexander," with a smile.

"And what of the 360-degree radiation problem?" Fletcher says.

"It seems that we can't solve this problem says Isabella, the only solution to that is that all the ships must return to planet Earth for a refit."

It was a throwaway remark but it resonated with everyone. Was that the best plan to come back and then leave again with the light drives finished and all the ships fully protected?

The remark hangs in the room like a bad smell.

"That is a possibility," says Henri, "with the light drive, they are less than six hours away. Three things then, first a time schedule for the canisters that includes all the necessary computer programs from Palma if you can't do it, second, explore the drone idea so contact Palma on that too and third..." Henri pauses for effect...and IRIS felt a huge spike in Alexandre's anxiety.

"And 3," said IRIS, flashing the thought to Henri, "we will be back to you on that. Thank you for your presentations. It falls far below what we expected. Update us in two weeks, Michael."

They leave for the airport.

14.35 The brief to Du Pont

"That went well," said Michael, "we have an excellent instruction to move forward. Alexandre, you liaise with Palma, Isabella, there are some problems with canister deployment to solve, I think they noticed this and Thomas, excellent work. Any questions?"

"You are joking, aren't you Michael? It was a disaster. We looked inept, incompetent and under-resourced and they clearly suspect us. I shall be surprised if we are not all arrested within days. Not only that but Alexandre was practically pi***** himself."

"Thank you, Isabella, I will consider that. Mary, something? Nothing? all good. Okay, let's go."

Alexandre was indeed now very nervous, there was Kostyantyn's message via their mutual friend, and the robots were very scary, he would have to think very carefully before helping Kostyantyn.

15.30 onboard private flight back to NASA

"We all felt something from Alexandre," said Fletcher, "what was that?"

"Yes, I decided not to probe his thoughts at this stage, but he was very nervous and it was not about his presentation," said IRIS, "and which was beyond useless," said Abe.

"We all felt it," said Henri, Abe smiled.

Fletcher feels a little left out of it.

"I did not have your ability to read minds but, I am very sensitive and I noticed his discomfort. But that doesn't make him guilty of anything."

The mood in the plane was gloomy as it became clear the mission would be better served if it returned to planet Earth.

"Let's wait until we return to Pasadena before we pick this up again," said Abe.

"Arrival at 'Bob Hope' Airport in 5 minutes, sorry for the diversion from LAX, some protesters on the runway, belts and seats up, you know the drill," says the captain.

October 14th NASA Conference Chamber 12 09.30

Kostyantyn was brought to NASA under guard; Aleksander and Fedir were also there in different rooms. Abe, Henri and IRIS were in the room.

"Hi, Kostyantyn," said Abe, "we trust that you are well and recovered from your injuries. Tea water, coffee?"

"No, thank you."

"Okay, well, we are here because we need information from you. We are happy to negotiate but we need the information. We know that you contacted Alexander. We know you are the saboteur and we know that there is a random aspect to your betrayal." Abe smiles.

"We wish to know all that you do. It does not matter about chance or random occurrences, it is what it is and we will take care of it."

Kostyantyn felt a chill in his spinal column.

"Your choice," said Henri, "is this."

"Tell us all about the sabotage in minute detail, voluntarily, or IRIS will enter your mind and after that, you will be a vegetable. What would you like to do?" Abe said with a smile and a little bow.

Konstantyn's life flashed before him.

"Think about it, we will come back, and they left the room. Oh and please, help yourself to coffee, water or tea."

Kostyantyn looked at the door, it opened again.

"I forgot to mention," said Abe, "the facilities are through there and indicates a frosted glass door. Please make yourself comfortable."

Konstantyn got up and went to the door. It was a comfortable living room with chairs and sofas, TV with internet and telephone, another door, also frosted glass, opens to a bedroom and private bathroom. There are fresh clothes, toiletries, towels and lotions and underwear and pyjamas. There was a red bell in every room. Konstantyn doesn't believe it.

Conference Room **14, 10.30**

IRIS, Henri and Leroy enter Fedir's room. They say exactly the same thing they did to Konstyantyn.

This time Leroy gives the additional information. There are the same facilities, living room, bedroom and bathroom and clothes etc.

Conference Chamber 15, 11.30

The same, exactly for Aleksander, and Leroy with the additional information.

Rooms 12, 14, 15, 12.30 Hours (the Same Scene)

A knock at the door. There is a waiter. "Would you like some lunch? Here is a menu, I will be back soon."

Aleksander, Fedir and Konstyantyn all choose from the menu.

16.00 hours (the same scene)

"Do you want some afternoon tea?"

19.30 hours (the same scene)

"Dinner menu."

10.30 hours

The telephone rings in every room.

"Breakfast will be at 08.00 am, good night, ring the bell if you need something. Anything at all. Sleep well," said the voice.

15 October NASA Conference Room 9a 0 7.30

Abe, Henri, IRIS and Fletcher discuss day 1.

"What are you thinking?" Fletcher said, wearing yellow nails and a large coffee.

Abe, Henri and IRIS all smile at him.

"The plan today," says IRIS, "is to talk with Fedir, she is the most militant."

"Just Fedir," said Leroy, "why not all of them?"

"She is the most difficult but she does not have all the information. The others know this and they will let them talk to each other. That does not matter. We wait, they will make a mistake and if we need to read Fedir's thoughts or any of them…" IRIS did not finish the sentence.

Rooms 12, 14, 15, 08.00 Hours (the Same to All)

Knock on doors. Waiters bring tea, coffee, water, butter croissants and preserves.

"If you want a breakfast 'full English', I will take your instructions now. Moreover, your colleagues are also in this corridor, you can meet with each other, the telephones are available, you can speak freely, the rooms are not locked, and there are no constraints. You could do whatever you wanted. Of course, the exits are locked. If you need anything, ring the bell."

Room 12 09.15 Hours.

They all met in Kostantyn's room. It was a strange meeting.

"You seem well," said Fedir to Kostantyn.

"Thank you, but we have a very serious problem," said Kostantyn.

"Well, you do, but Fedir and I, we don't know everything," says Aleksander.

"Isn't it strange, all this 5-star treatment?" Fedir said with a frown.

"They are on the back foot, they need us," said Kostyantyn.

"Well, I did my own special tricks," says Fedir.

"And so did I," said Aleksander, "and they won't find them. You're not the only one with an agenda, Kostantyn," Fedir said.

They all looked at each other; each was totally surprised by the others revelations.

"I don't believe their threats, which are clearly illegal for one thing and I don't think they can do it anyway," Fedir said. "We can each say what we all know and keep quiet about the rest. That will present a consistent face.

Personally, I am convinced that robots can and do want to harm us, if we do not tell them what they want to know. The problem is the random events."

"The problem, Kostantyn," said Fedir, "is that you've lost your nerve."

"You are both wrong, the problem is that it is an old campaign and it is no longer relevant." Aleksander shook his head and sighed. Fedir got up and left without another word.

Conference Room 14, 15.30 st., 15 October 2044

Fedir was not at all troubled, she was not convinced by the threats, in fact, she felt very important. She was very mistaken.

She changes into jeans and a sweater, cashmere in grey.

There is a knock on the door.

"Good afternoon, Fedir."

At the door were IRIS, Elena Marquez, and Abe.

"We came for a little chat with you," says IRIS. "Are you comfortable?"

"Would you like to tell us all that you know about the sabotage?" Elena says.

"I don't know much, Kostyantyn was the principal of our little schema."

"You know that people are dead and the mission is in trouble," said Abe.

"They deserve what they get."

"Do you want to tell us everything you know?" Elena said.

"Not a chance."

"Why not?" Abe said.

"I don't believe you and, I don't care."

"Last chance," says IRIS.

Fedir called the others. "Let's meet up tomorrow, make sure our ducks are in line. Meanwhile, F*** them."

Conference Room 14, 08.00 a.m., October 16th

Kostyantyn and Aleksander knocked on the door and entered. They all needed to chat. Fedir wore blue jeans and a cashmere sweater in grey, she was reading an article. She did not look up at Kostantyn and Aleksander. They took their coffee and sat down. Fedir remained staring down.

Then a wave of panic strikes Kostantyn as he realises that the article is upside down. He talks to Fedir again. No answer, he taps her on the knee. She looks up. Her eyes were completely black, he dropped his coffee. Aleksander, just stared. They get up and leave without a word.

The doors of 12 and 15 close, at the end of the corridor the double door opens, two orderlies enter with a wheelchair and stop at room 14.

Conference 9A 17 October, 10.30 a.m.

Abe, IRIS, Henri, Fletcher and Marquez are all assembled for the meetings to discuss the next move.

"Well, with the approval of President Marika, we have our vegetable and we have some answers," Abe said. "It is tragic but was necessary."

"Let's not dwell on it," said Fletcher, "the fact is that we now have choices to make. It's clear Aleksander and Kostyantyn will speak but it's also clear that neither had an overall plan."

"We now know," said Abe, "the Vostov 4 spacecraft will suffer catastrophic damage on 24 February 2045, also that the Chinese ship, 'Lie-Long' (beautiful dragon) will suffer a disastrous systems failure in the new year, the year of the Wood Ox, 木牛年"

"And," says IRIS, "there is the problem of 'Palma Systems' and Alexandre Jocovic."

Henri makes a decision.

"We will contact Marika and the other heads of state."

11.30 a.m.

"Gerald, it's Henri, we need to talk with Marika."

Du Pont, 30 October

Henri, Abe, IRIS, Vincent and Leroy were all there. The same representation from Du Pont. "Welcome," said Michael, "you know everyone, Mary, Thomas, Alexander and Isabella."

"Sure, thank you, Michael," said Abe, "maybe you want to update us."
Mary took over.

"We have a prototype canister and a screen for your inspection, it's 1/4 scale, please, follow me." Everyone gets up and follows Mary outside.

"The screen is 1/20th scale (3 metre × 3 metre) but you will see how it works."

There was a large crowd of spectators, Isabella was holding a computer.

"Stay back everyone, 10, 9, 8, 7, 6, 5, 4, 3, 2, 1, go."

The canister opens slowly, four small drones emerge and fly at a height of 10 metres, where they perform acrobatics before flying back to the canister.

The presentation was a complete disaster, no better than what you can see in the park on a Sunday. There was a hushed silence.

"I suggest we go back to the conference room," said Abe. It was an 8-minute walk.

"Tea, coffee water," says Michael; Abe, Vincent and Leroy take coffee.

IRIS was already there, only the team of Du Pont were astonished by this.

Mary looks embarrassed, Thomas looks smug, Isabella looks mortified. Alexandre looks very nervous.

"You know that we are NASA right?" Vincent said.

"Let me explain," said Isabella. "The screens and canister are easy; the hard part is the computer program. Perhaps Alexander can update us."

Alexander now looks in full panic. IRIS stares at him. He swallows hard and plays his card.

"The thing is, we need Kostyantyn and we can't find him."

"What for?"

"He is the only one who can write the program."

"You know that we are NASA?" Vincent says again.

Everyone is looking uncomfortable.

"We need him, you need him," said Alexandre, now sweating profusely.

"Let me enlighten you," said IRIS. "We have him. What we wish to know from you Alexandre is what you know about the sabotage of the mission."

Alexandre blanched; the Du Pont team all looked at him. IRIS is at the back of the room. She appears instantaneously 150 millimetres in front of Alexandre's face. He fainted.

Isabella throws water over his face and watches it dribble down his cheeks. He stirs.

"Tell us all that you know or you will become like Fedir. You can ask Kostyantyn about Fedir."

"That's not what we expected," Michael said in shock.

"No it is not," said Abe, but it is a matter of national security and we will take Alexandre with us. Elena Marquez and two other police officers came to the door and arrested him and handcuffed him.

"Well," said Abe, "now we have a lot to discuss."

Zulu, 1 November

Since the incident on 23 September and the 'bon voyage' message, the spaceship has been on tenterhooks. Without warning, the annoying sound of the emergency horn blares throughout the ship.

"What the F**** now?" Mlungisi said, looking anxiously at all the status indicators.

The gimbal port, number 4 is flashing red. The robots are sent immediately and all the systems are isolate. They watch in horror as the number 4 pod escapes and gets stuck in the number 3 before it spins-off in space accompanied by hundreds of pieces of debris.

"Make a call to NASA," Abebe said.

NASA, 6 Hours Later

Vincent le Grange11, head of NASA receive the message from Zulu at 15.30 hours. It reads: This is Abebe, another disaster, but fortunately, without injury. What do you recommend? Continue, stop and wait?

Vincent calls Henri.

"Henri, it's Vincent. There was more sabotage on Zulu."

"OK, Vincent, the situation is that we have all the saboteurs and we also have their information but it is clear that something will happen automatically. It is programmed in and it's deadly. Our plan is to equip an evacuation ship, tow it to the fleet then bring them back here. We have a small globe that we can convert, but we do not have the light drives yet and the best guess is another three weeks. Please send this message on to them but of course," says Henri, "send the message but only if you can do all of this in three weeks, okay, Vincent?"

"Okay, Henri," and puts the phone down.

11.00 a.m., 2 November NASA Conference Room 9a

Space shuttles were built in Palmdale California by Rockwell International. There were six in total.

Challenger was destroyed in 1986 after launch 10th, Columbia was destroyed in re-entry in 2003 and Enterprise, the first, a glider really, was launched from the back of a Boeing 747 and was disassembled in 1977. The remaining three are Atlantis 1985–2011, Discovery 1984–2011 and Endeavour 1992–2011.

The room, which had seen many strange meetings, was now full. Marika, Gerald, Vincent, Abe, Fletcher, Henri, IRIS, the 2 Ruperts and the 2 BERT plus

Charlotte, back from vacation. There is one link per globe to the leaders of the other spaceships, Russia, South America, France, China, Great Britain, Voyager and Independence. Henri addresses them all.

"Only two months since our last meeting here and now, we have very difficult choices to make. There are two main problems, one Europium and two the light drive and now, if that were not enough, the possibility that the mission may be destroyed by the latent effects of sabotage, at any time and without warning. Zulu, is on its way here. It's suffered a second incident and awaits advice."

"What are our choices?" The Russian President says.

"Well, little really," said Henri, "your spaceship is likely to be attacked on 24 February; the Chinese in the new year. We do not need the umbrella screens if we will pick them all up and get them back here before December but the size of the light drive necessary to open a hole in space for the spaceships is larger than the capacity of the shuttle bay to carry. At the moment, we are stuffed."

"And," said Vincent, "at this point, we do not yet have enough Europium."

"What does Marika suggest?"

"It's radical but, our best idea is to abandon all the spaceships except one, transfer all the people to that one and pick up Zulu on the way back. So, take our time and then go back and collect the other ships, if they are still in one piece."

"We have to vote on which ships and of course, eventually the decision will be for the ships, not us," said Marika.

The Voting Procedure.

12.00 hours, several votes but no decision.

"Give them a break for lunch and get back here at 2.00 p.m.," said Henri.

Only Marika, Gerald, Abe, Vincent, Charlotte and Fletcher need food but all postpone that to go for the coffee.

"It's difficult," says Marika, "seems to me the best choice will be Independence or Beautiful Forest (Belle Foret) they have the most capacity."

"Okay," said Henri, and Abe, Fletcher, and Charlotte agree.

"I think, Voyager and Belle Foret," said Vincent, "let's see at 14.00 hours."

14.00 hours

"Welcome, all," said Marika, "have you made your choice?"

The Chinese were the first to speak.

"We do not have a total agreement but we have a choice."

"What is it?" Marika said.

"Voyager and Beautiful Foret, both have excellent facilities, less than Russia but very importantly, no defects so far and two is better than one."

Vincent smiles, Abe bows and everyone else, with one voice shouts in agreement.

"Well," said Henri, "two it is. I have some changes to make."

"And be quick about it," said IRIS, flashing her very large eyes.

The Light Drive

Henri had developed the light drive for the small shuttle of the USS Independence. It was about the size of a V8 engine and projected a beam that opened a hole in space. In this case, 50 metres in diameter. Now Henri needs a light drive capable of opening a hole of 2820 metres (the full size of the Boomerang class ships and which is the largest configuration) so 3,500 minimum for safety, so 7 or 8 times larger.

The size of the shuttle Endeavour cargo hold is 4.5 metres × 18 metres.

Henri decided to make each light-speed drive from a ball of 2 metres in diameter with focus tubes of 1 metre × 300 mm, conical shape, 5 per ball.

The Europium is used at the rate of 6 tons per month per drive and therefore, immediately Henri needs 48 tons for the main ship, the others can follow in the wake of Belle Foret.

The power cells that contain the Europium resemble watch batteries except that they are larger, two metres in diameter by 300 mm high. Used discs will be recycled. At some point perhaps.

Henri is 12 tons short at this time but has around six weeks to go. He is not worried.

Gabriella writes some more notes. The globe seems anxious to receive the information, it's pulsating. She skates off with Meeka dodging in and out of her strides, makes another pass and throws the pages at the globe which absorbs them with a little shudder and a brief flash of numbers that scroll at incredible speed within it. They return to the table, they seem to have been away for quite some time.

Zulu, 3 November
21.30 hours.

The Zulu Bridge is huge, smaller than a Russian ship, but it has an atrium which is spectacular. On duty, navigation, Commander Lieutenant Bill Botha, pilot, Malaika Savanna, co-pilot Barack Mulele (the man who flies), communications Robert McCarthy, an American.

"Bill, incoming message from NASA," said Robert with a frown. It says:

Zulu, it's NASA. The world leaders here have decided, or suggest to you, that we bring back three spaceships, Zulu, Voyager and Belle Floret. The others will be abandoned. We will be with you on 17 December or later. For now, continue on your present track and speed. NASA out.

"Well," said Abebe, who had just arrived on deck.

The good thing about Zulu was the shuttle bridge. It allows a shuttle to land without difficulty. In case there was another occurrence of sabotage on board, it was decided to practice escape to the pods, but not all at the same time. With 4,000 people on board, that's 80 shuttles of 50 capacities each.

The atrium spans four decks; it's bright, colourful, and noisy with escalators, shopping, and food courts and is now full of people. Everyone was paying attention. Abebe was at the lectern.

"We have news from NASA, it's interesting, essentially we would be collected by the spacecraft Belle Forêt and USS Voyager by 17 December which will have already been prepared for the return journey at light-speed. In the meantime, we are focused on our own sub-light return to planet Earth. If you have a question, raise your hand."

There is a forest of hands.

"OK, I suggest that we take 10 and see if that covers all."

"It's very difficult, you, James, I think work in the lemon tree café, your question?"

"Will the ship collapse?"

50% of the hands go down.

"It is possible, but we know the risks, well, most of them, but there is the problem of random sabotage, the details of which clearly we do not know."

Three hands remain.

"Sarah, you are with the pharmacy, yes?" She nods. "Your question, please."

"Thank you, Abebe, my question is, do you think, if we go back to Earth, should we stay?"

Two hands were lowered.

"I think that if we get back, all of us that is, then maybe the mission will become one of exploration only, not escape."

"You mean like 'Star Trek'."

"Yes, like 'Star Trek'."

It was a pivotal moment. The idea is that the mission can be reformed from a disaster into an adventure. Of course, they will need weapons and the Omniscient would not allow it. Maybe their new home can be where the portal went. IRIS will know. There was a shiver of excitement throughout the ship.

Gabriella was now penning notes at a very fast rate.

RECORD 7, 10 November 2044, The Andromeda Galaxy

The galaxy is about 2.5 billion miles (770 kiloparsecs) from planet Earth.

Right ascension east: 00 h 42m 44.3 s

Declination: 41 degrees 16 min 9 sec

Audry, Oneson, Rupert IRIS and Henri chose this galaxy for Earth 2.

It will collide with the Milky Way in about 4.5 billion years. Quite a way off. It is a blue offset galaxy which is approaching the Milky Way at 110km per second. It was detected in 1999, event ref PA-99-N2. Of course, the Omnicients already know this.

They had considered but discounted galaxy ALESS 073.1 discovered by Dr Lelli and his team in 2023 using the Atacama Large millimetre array or ALMA, as it appeared to defy the laws of known physics. This was a pity. It would have been just right.

Gabriella had a lot to say about this and wrote for an hour, or perhaps a year or more or was it seconds? She threw the notes at the globe which, as usual, absorbed them and flashed some numbers at her.

The complex in Andromeda is a series of domes each capable of accommodating 500 people in total, therefore, 100 domes for a total of 50,000 people.

The arrival station resembles the space station on planet Earth, a large tube 100 high × 30 metres in diameter with docking ports for the 100 transport vessels arriving from locations all over the world. Set in a radial plan, 10 ports every 10 metres. At the bottom of the central tube are the geodesic domes, five in total again in radial plan with connection tubes to each of 10-meter diameter.

Each dome includes five floors, three above the ground and two below.

In total, there are 3,333 support units or cells as they are affectionately known, per floor, 50 square metres each, including a bed, chair, table and a toilet. Basic but entirely liveable in the short term.

The geometry is of a central tube, that's the docking station, five tubes radiate out to domes, three floors above and two below ground. Further tubes and domes are planned once the station is up and running.

In the central floor area of the vertical access tube is an atrium with vending machines as was so typical in Japan. The cells are mainly for sleeping. Each of the floors is three metres high. The top of the dome has fewer cells, more below and more again at the ground. The inner circles, deprived of natural light, have light pipes as well as artificial light. The below-ground levels contain all the equipment necessary for the function of the complex. These basement floors, two of them, are five metres high with storage for very heavy equipment, materials to build more domes, environmental systems, workshops, robots, shuttle bays with elevators on the ground. In basement 1 are the hospital, library, scientific laboratories, restaurants, gymnasiums and leisure, education and administration and cinemas.

The globes are located on a 12-acre grid, 5 × 4, 240 acres complete.

The setup is:

Dome 1 accommodation plus central admin, shuttle control and hospital.

Dome 2 accommodation plus leisure.

Dome 3 more scientific accommodation, horticulture and gene bank, survey and cartography.

Dome 4 accommodation plus biblioteque or library.

Dome 5 accommodation plus education.

Each dome has the same layout as basement 2, parts and machinery, heavy equipment, catering, cinemas, shuttle bays and robots.

The idea is for the complex to develop more radials and domes when necessary. At this time, the complex when full will cover some 500 hectares, (1.93 sq. miles), it is affectionately called the Octopus.

They are in a valley with a gentle stream and lush vegetation and beyond a snowy mountain. The air is fresh and there is the sound of birds. Apart from the strange colour, the sky is green, the trees are blue, there are 3 moons, the sun is yellow with a red stripe and the day is 29 hours long, it seems like paradise.

What could possibly go wrong?

The Omniscient and Audry have provided all the equipment, housing and machinery necessary for the development of the planet.

There is also a control centre with holographic maps of the planet and galaxies, including the Milky Way and planet Earth. Other planets in the Andromeda system have been identified for future terraformation.

There was also detailed information about the geology and it was clear that Earth 2 was very complex.

One of the first problems on arrival was to organise a structure for their society. The other problem was motivation, with so many things found, what's the challenge?

Oneson and Audry had considered sending the portal ships back to Earth, maybe others would be inclined to go but on balance, with no point in a return to Earth where millennia will have passed, Oneson decides to keep them. You don't know what will happen later.

James, Delphine and Marcus, all scientists and natural leaders, with Oneson, Benton and Rupert 1 form the basis of the council. The portals already identified the most suitable people for specific tasks. There was no hierarchy, just function, and it was not rigid, people could change when they desired and were there a natural rotation so that everyone would be able eventually to do everything. A big ambition. Of course, some were specialists, doctors, scientists, teachers and there were robots and Ruperts, a hundred of them. It was Utopia. What could possibly go wrong?

In the planet archive, evidence of a complex of pre-existing derelict domes was discovered. It lay just seven hundred kilometres away. At cruise shuttle speed of 350 kph, the journey would take a couple of hours. It was worth a look.

James, Delphine and Marcus took a shuttle to explore the domes. It was an uneventful flight except when the sand arose. Comms went down at 50 miles from Octopus station and there was no way to send a mayday.

18 November

Feeling slightly uneasy, there should have been contact with the shuttle every 30 minutes, Oneson sent a drone.

The drone had an uneventful flight, no sand, which was blessing beautiful purple water that changes like the terrain changes colour, red, and green, yellow, purple. Onboard instruments indicate that the complex of domes is now just 200 km away, half an hour. Real-time visual information is transmitted to the Octopus base.

25.00 hours Geodome 3

Oneson, Benton, Francis, Gerome, and Rupert 1 are all gathered around the screen. Wesley is in bed. The 29-hour day takes a little getting used to it. The images were amazing. Oneson congratulates Francis.

At 5 km, the domes are very clear, the drone stops 30 metres from the edge. The shuttle is in pieces, surrounded by 6 large 1.5-meter-long silver ants. Three more arrive with some more pieces of the wreck.

"The guardians," says Oneson, "are still here and working. I did not expect that after 5 Millenia. I thought this was very firmly in the past."

Francis and Gerome are looking at the screens, Francis drops his coffee. Gerome just looks at the screen with his mouth wide open.

"We need answers," said Francis, attempting to regain her composure.

Oneson quickly fills in the gaps.

"The Omniscient thought it would be a good idea, 5,000,000 years ago, at the time of their last intervention on planet Earth, to form a colony in another galaxy, and people it with a human-like species," said Oneson.

"And was it?" Gerome said.

"We'll see," said Rupert.

The silver ants are making quick clicks; Rupert 1 is very attentive.

"This is the situation," says Rupert. "Marcus and James are dead, Delphine is wounded but not seriously, the shuttle was knocked down by the sandstorm, it is common, the water disappears, the purple sand forms large clouds and…"

"Ask what happened to the previous human-like colony," said Oneson.

More clicks.

"The planet killed them," says Rupert 1.

"Ask when it will be safe to send another shuttle."

More clicks.

"In six months," says Rupert 1, "the silver ants will take care of Delphine and the drone can be used to communicate indefinitely."

Oneson was worried; the Omniscient had not disclosed this information. Why not?

This information potentially threatens the entire mission.

Zulu, 18 November

Abebe was very optimistic that Henri could find them in time, but December was getting closer. In case of emergency, their plan was to leave Zulu by the shuttles.

11.00 am, 18 November NASA Conference Room 9a

Henri, Abe, Leroy, Rupert, and IRIS were all in the conference to receive the call from Zulu, scheduled for 11.15 hours EST.

A blip on the line…

"It's Abebe here, we hope that everything is good for you to come for us. We decided to check the escape pods, just in case. We will send another message later. Abebe out."

Leroy was the first to speak.

"It seems to me, if they go ahead with this idea, it is possible it will cause a malfunction, and then what?"

"Maybe not a problem," said Henri, "but on the other hand, maybe you're right."

"IRIS, Rupert?" Henri said.

"We know that there is nothing planned by the saboteurs but the possibility exists of something random," says IRIS, "and it could be a disaster."

"Do we all agree?" Henri said.

"Yes." All agree.

"Send the message," says Abe and now we have to return to the problem of Europium, three tons short. "A little less than four weeks to go, we are struggling."

Zulu 19 November

The NASA message arrived at 5:00 p.m. last night but it is scrambled, some text is missing, it reads as follows:

"Zulu, your message was received. We have discussed…we agree that you must…activate…pods. We will be with you by 15 December. Good luck and see you soon. NASA out."

Captain Mlungisi Manqoba and co-driver Sebastian Ritter discuss the message.

"There are gaps in the transmission but it seems clear, we have to go before the 15th," Sebastian said, "I'll inform Abe."

"Okay," says Mlungisi. "We can run the tests for 09.00 tomorrow."

09.00 hours

Abebe decided to be cautious. NASA's message had shortcomings and they could be negative. He changed the plan so that the test would include 15 shuttles only and spread over five days. A test, wait three hours, then another and wait and the final for that day, then, the next day the same.

"Send the test plan to NASA please, Mlungisi."

The Zulu Bridge was calm but busy. The first emergency shuttle was checked and checked again. Twenty people volunteered. The plan was to sound the alarm, 20 go to the shuttle and launch. Before the launch, the communications announced that **it was an exercise. There was an air of expectation.**

Each shuttle was capable of carrying 50 people, but they were setting limits. Groups of 20 people were stationed at different places around the spacecraft waiting for alarms.

"Let's go," said Abebe.

Sebastian Ritter raises the alarm. Horns, red lights and messages, **abandon ship,** sounded around the spacecraft. It would take 11 minutes to launch Pod 1. Everyone has been trained in navigation. Sophie, a pharmacist, was in control, her instructions were to circle the ship for 15 minutes, then back.

At 13.30 hours, pod 2 piloted by Patrick, a qualified mechanic. Launches without problems.

At 16.30 hours, pod 3 piloted by Hubert Mandisa, no problems.

"Send a message to NASA," says Abebe, "three tests, all with success."

20 November

Day 2. Horns, red lights and messages, **abandon ship,** sounded around the ship. 3 tests without problems.

21 November

Day 3. Horns, red lights and messages, **abandon ship**, rang around the ship. 3 tests without problems.

22 November, day 4

"So far so good," said Abebe, "when you are ready, Sebastian."

All was going well, nerves were calm. Horns, red lights and messages, **abandon ship,** sounded around the ship. Three tests without problems.

23 November, day 5

The same procedure.

Test 1 without problem, test 2 without problem, test 3, the last. Sebastian Ritter is the pilot.

"I will go around for another 15 minutes."

21.00 hours.

"Zulu, it's pod 15 on finals."

"Okay, pod 15; approach your tube 19, please."

"100 metres, 80, 60, 30 all good…"

There was an orange ball of fire 20 metres from tube 19…Everything went quiet.

Abebe looked speechless, a second later.

"Tube 19?"

"We have them, the fire is out, the doctors are there."

Abebe arrived in three minutes, the scene at tube 19 was quiet. People were receiving treatment for burns. Sebastian was on a chair with the other victims.

"What happened?" Abebe said, looking with concern for his friend.

It was strange, all was good, all green; then a message appeared on the screens.

It said, 'Have a nice day.'

Palma Systems are subcontractors to the manufacturers of nacelles 10, 9, 8, 7, 6, you can imagine what came next, the instruments and the propellant catch fire, smoke everywhere and we receive some burns but then the automatic suppression fire puts everything out. It's strange, the systems work, but slowly, hence the burns.

"Rest for now, everyone is safe, that's the important thing, we will talk tomorrow."

24 November

The hope was that all would be well after 14 successful shuttle tests, but now there was the possibility that other ships would be compromised. Abebe sent a message to NASA.

"The thing is," Sebastian said, "it could have been a catastrophe, it wasn't!"

The mood on board the ship was gloomy, the spirits were low.

"What I don't understand," said Mlungisi, "is the timing, why now?"

"It's sabotage without doubt," said Abebe.

"There must be a start point, if we find the beginning of the fire, perhaps we will discover the cause," said Sebastian.

"Exactly," said Abebe, "let's go-go-go, a lot to do."

25 November 17.53 h

The technicians have covered the starting point of the fire, a power coupling in duct number Z49908>PSP>nacelle.

"It's Palma Systems Pasadena, without a doubt," said Abebe. "Send an emergency message to Henri immediately, please, Mlungisi."

NASA Conference Room 9a 26 November, 01.19 Hours

Henri, IRIS, Fletcher and Abe were all staring at the message screen.

"This came in a little earlier," said Fletcher, "I thought I would allow you a little more sleep," said Fletcher, with a smile towards Abe.

"Thank you, Leroy, very kind." Fletcher was not passionate about being called Leroy. He gave a little bow and a smile.

"The thing is," said Henri, "it is impractical to remove each relay in each exhaust pod at this time. The best thing is to wait until the fleet returns to planet Earth, assuming we do."

25.00 hours Geodome 3 November 30

With the news that the mission to save Delphine will have to wait until May next year, 2045, life at the Octopus base has settled into a routine.

Benton undertook the construction of the new domes. The materials were all there and as good as the robots; there were many hands available for the tasks. The first concern was why the previous humanity was killed off. It is clear that Delphine would be able to discover the answer when she was well.

Delphine

She had woken up in a bright and spacious room, her head hurt and her ribs were sore but other than that, she was ok, a little thirsty but ok.

When the silver ants arrived, she was scared but their clicks were calming. She went back to sleep. When she woke up, the clicks made total sense.

"I am guardian number 60, I will take care of you, do not be afraid."

She went back to sleep.

"Hello, Delphine, how are you?"

"What happened, what are you?"

"I am a Guardian, there are a lot of us."

"How long?"

"50,000 years, but the time does not matter. We were switched off when the previous humanity conducted themselves in the same way as planet Earth has just done. They all died. We were reactivated when the new portal was opened, this November. We have waited for you. If this new experiment is a success, it will be number 300 on this planet, a number of cosmic significance. But you will not understand that."

"Why did it fail?"

"They all failed, cruelty and lack of respect for nature."

"What if we do the same?"

"You will suffer the same fate."

"What can I do?"

"When you are completely recovered, I will show you."

"How is it that I understand you?"

"It is a translation implant, very easy."

"Can I contact the Octopus base?"

"Of course, the drone will do it and we will activate the transmitter here. No problem."

"I have a billion questions."

"Yes, ask at any time," says Guardian 60 with bow.

"I'll call you **George,** if that's ok?"

"OK, and you are Delphine."

Delphine and George begin to explore the complex. Ants and other robots are attacking vegetation with a machine that looks like a large disc or two cookies with a space between them and many legs. The cookie picks up vegetation, moves it towards a free space on the ground and it disappears.

Within three days, the complete complex is clear with grass walkways. The sound of running water and birdsong fills the air. It's paradise. Delphine calls the Octopus base.

Gabriella scribbles some more notes, the cookies are the same; the plan the same. What will change in this version? The globe eats the notes. She wonders why she knows all this.

11.50 hours 3 December Geodome 3

"Purple base, it is Delphine."

"Hello, Delphine, it's Gerome."

"Gerome, I need to talk to Oneson."

Three minutes pass.

"Delphine, how are you?"

"I am good, but I have a lot to tell you."

"I suspect you have," said Oneson.

"The ants are the guardians. The one that helped me is number 60. Now I call him George. He is 50,000 years old but the complex is 5,000,000 years old. It's a little confusing but there have been many experiments here. All failed. Also, there are other robots, cookies, the same I suspect as those that were eating the buildings on our planet. At the moment, they are cleaning up the vegetation which then disappears. The immediate previous humanity, 50, 000 years ago, was killed by this planet because it did not respect the planet. This is now our present danger."

Delphine was out of breath, she was waiting for Oneson's answer.

"Delphine, we are very happy and relieved that you and ok. We have some questions for you if that's ok?"

"OK, I'm fine."

"First, what happened to the bodies of Marcus and James?"

"The cookies have erased the wreck, but this is all I know. I'll ask George."

"OK, good."

"Second, can you explore the complex?"

"I will ask of George."

"OK good. This is very important, do you realise that you are on your own for six months?"

"Yes, but George takes care of me and I understand everything he says, thanks to an implant."

"OK, Delphine, call us 24/7 as necessary. In any case, we will call you every week. Talk soon."

Oneson was very worried, Delphine was alone for six months, the cookies were here, and she had an alien implant.

NASA Conference Room 9a 3 December.

Henri, IRIS, Fletcher and Abe were examining the progress of the light propulsion drives. Less than two weeks to go before the hour to leave.

"A quarter ton to go, more globes to make, everything is fine, we will be ready to launch in a week," says Abe.

Charlotte enters.

"Hello, Charlotte, good to see you," said Abe.

"I would like to say you need another pilot."

"Yes and a very good pilot."

"And that's me, you were about to say."

"Yes, welcome aboard," Abe said with a smile and bow.

"Our plan," said Henri, "is to take the three shuttles, Atlantis, Discovery and Endeavour, load them all with the light propulsion for the three spaceships, Zulu, Voyager and Belle Floret and abandon the others. Everyone, Russians, Vostov 4 (востоков 4), Lie-Long 美丽的 (Beautiful Dragon), Chinese, Madame Juliette Francais and Great Britain, Arc Royal 6, will be moving to USS Voyager and Belle Floret. This is the most difficult phase but if all goes well, the journey is only about six hours and we will pick up Zulu on our return to planet Earth."

"And," said Abe, "Zulu is in trouble at this moment. We hope there is no problem before we arrive."

"Well," said Fletcher, "if we are to meet our 17 December launch, there is a lot to do. I have prepared a checklist, everyone is working on it."

Fletcher puts the list on the screen.

3 December today.

Action NASA

1. Full action test flights of the shuttle, Atlantis, Discovery, Endeavour certify pilots. One is doubtful.

Check the Europium is on target.

2. Propulsion light.

4 December
Action Henri

1. Complete flight plans.
2. Send information and coordinate space and time to Zulu, Voyager and Belle Foret.

5 December
Action Fletcher

1. Issue the legal opinion of sabotage to Palma Systems.

Action Charlotte

1. Take Atlantis and the team to the space station to check the docking procedure.

Action IRIS

1. Perform checks with BERTS.

6 December
Action NASA

1. Still checking that Europium is on target.

Action Fletcher

2. Run the security controls on each person working on the project.

7 December
Action Fletcher and IRIS

1. Lock the shuttle site.

Action IRIS

2. Start the countdown 240,239,238, each item, location, every hour. Check! Check! Check!

"Thanks, Fletcher," said Henri, "I think that covers everything. There are hundreds of people involved in the mission, actually 691 in total. All are to be verified, a big task but what worries me is the transfer of the people from the ships that are to be abandoned."

"Also," said Abe, "Zulu's problem may yet become difficult."

"Okay," said Henry, "maybe we should fix Zulu first and not on the way home. We will prepare one shuttle with a light propulsion system for Zulu plus a team to install and drop off én route."

"Good idea," said Abe, "some new calculations please, Henri," he said with a smile and his usual bow.

Zulu 4 December

There are no problems, all systems work properly, and morale is good, they just had to wait for their rescue.

"13 days to go," says Mlungisi to Abebe, "let's keep our fingers crossed."

NASA 10 December

Seven days to go, everything is on the right track, temporal and spatial coordinates were sent to Zulu, Voyager and Belle Foret.

On security, there were five names of interest, now awaiting interviews in Chambers **12, 14, 15.**

Room 12 a 09.00 Hours

Henri, IRIS, Fletcher and Marquez plus a BERT, were all in the room at the head of an oval table. Tea, coffee and croissants plus water, orange juice and some sliced lemon were on a credenza. The three, all American were sitting at the other end. They all look very nervous.

"What are we doing here?" An overweight Texan said.

"You had filled out a questionnaire," said Fletcher with a smile, "and there is a problem with that."

"What problem?" The Texan said. "It was an easy questionnaire."

"Well," said Fletcher, "actually, the questions were very complex and from that we established that you had something to hide. Today, we find out what it is."

"Go ahead," says the Texan.

"Monsieur Granger," said IRIS, "I assure you that we will find out what it is."

The Texan felt a spike of fear.

"Please help yourself to coffee," said Fletcher.

"Miss Renard, you had a very interesting job at NASA. You coordinate the Europium supply with the installation of the discs. Is that true?" Fletcher said.

"Yes."

"It's a very important job is that also true?"

"Yes."

"And you, Mademoiselle Chopin, you are the one who would give the final approval, is that not also true?"

"Yes."

IRIS stands up and flashes her eyes at them for a second. Without destroying them, she established that Mademoiselle Renard and Mademoiselle Chopin were attempting a sabotage. They all feel a tingling sensation.

"Mademoiselle Chopin and Mademoiselle Renard, you will have a choice," said IRIS. "Mr Granger, you can go. Thank you for your contribution to the mission."

10.00 hours

It is clear that they, Chopin and Renard had conspired on their sabotage, it is not clear what it was or if Bertrand and Gotier were involved.

"Please, Sergent Marquez, give both the choice to tell us the truth or become a vegetable. Now we have Mr Bertrand and Miss Gotier to talk to."

Room 15 at 10.15 Hours

"Hello, Monsieur Bertrand and Miss Gotier, thank you for coming in to see us," says Fletcher. "Did you have breakfast? There is tea, coffee, water pastries and preserves. If you want something else, ring the bell. We will be back at 11.00 a.m."

Bertrand and Gotier looked at each other.

"It is impossible for them to know our plan," said Gotier.

"I agree," said Bertrand, "just keep Mum and shut up."

They were surprised at 11.00 a.m. when Fletcher returned with two robots and a police sergeant.

"Well," said Fletcher, "we know that you intend to sabotage the shuttles."

Fletcher grabs a coffee and looks at them.

"You are mad," said Bertrand, "there is no conspiracy."

"You have a choice," said IRIS, "you can tell us or become vegetables."

She blinked at them. They both felt a chill down their spines.

"Think about it, we'll be back at 12.00 o'clock," said Fletcher. "Please help yourselves to tea, coffee, water."

Room 15 a 12.00 h

Mademoiselle Gotier, Mademoiselle Chopin, Monsieur Renard and Monsieur Bertrand were all seated at the large table.

They were nervous and quiet. IRIS, Henri, Fletcher, Marquez and a BERT all enter the room.

"Good afternoon," said Fletcher, "we will now establish what your situation is. Who would like to go first?"

They all remain silent.

"OK," says sergeant Marquez, "permit me to show you a video clip of an interview at 15.30 hours, 15 October 2044."

They watched with total horror as Fedir became a vegetable. Mademoiselle Chopin faints.

"Miss Gotier, you know Fedir, is that true?"

"Yes."

"You know that…"

"Yes, a vegetable."

"What would you like to tell us?"

"Nothing."

Mademoiselle Chopin wakes up to the sight of the BERT next to her.

"You seem better," says Fletcher. "Would you like to tell us something?"

"Yes. We all met at MIT, including the team at Palma Systems. Kostyantyn was terrific, we admire him but we didn't have a score to settle, we are just anarchists and if we can cause damage, we will."

IRIS looked at Chopin.

"What did you do? Last chance."

"You don't bother me," said Chopin.

"Or any of us," said Bertrand, Gotier and Renard.

They all smile. It was a very surreal moment. They all stand, kiss and take a tablet from their pocket and swallow it. They raise their glasses of water.

"Long live anarchy," said Bertrand; they all sit down.

"IRIS, quickly, they are committing suicide."

IRIS looks at all of them, fractions of information, then blackness.

"They are dead," said IRIS.

"Sergeant Marquez, please, take care of it," said Henri.

They leave and reconvene in room 12.

Room 12 at 13.00 Hours

Abe, Henri, Fletcher and IRIS are all deciding what to do. Fletcher and Abe sit down with their coffee.

"I had fragments of thoughts, nothing detailed, but included is the Europium and the shuttles. Really, this is the jeopardy for the total mission."

"How much time do we have to change the Europium?" Fletcher asked.

"None, it's impossible," says Abe, "we will need another three or four months. Stocks are exhausted and mining is very difficult at this time."

"We can repair the shuttles, but the Europium screws us."

"We'll run with it for now, in seven days, we'll meet here," said Henri. "For now, we say nothing to Zulu, Belle Foret or Voyager. On the 16th, we take a bet, the biggest, on behalf of the lives of 47,700 people."

Voyager, 11 December

Captain Stephanie Miller had been studying the NASA information about the rendezvous, it is complicated.

Six days to go, it is very important that we arrive at the precise destination, says Stephanie to Vincent Chu.

"I think we have to arrive before the hour and stay put."

Stephane is English, 22 years old, tall and thin with black hair and grey eyes. Vincent Chu is Chinese/American with black hair and blue eyes, 23 years old and very handsome.

"There's a lot of things that bother me about the evacuation," said Stephanie, sipping her coffee from a large cup.

"Like what?" Vincent says.

"Well, time to move more than 15,000 people from here is one."

The bridge was noisy with the constant chatter of the crew and the communications. The other ships were close and soon to be abandoned; just Belle Floret and Voyager would join Zulu on the return.

"It will be easier if they can make two trips," says Stephanie.

"I think the one is very complicated, sabotage, Europium, we just have one shot and Zulu are already on their way, so, it is more than 15,000."

"But once they're here, it's six hours to come back to planet Earth, so let's just focus on that," Vincent said.

They remained silent for a while.

Room 12 at 13.00 Hours December 12th

Henri, IRIS, Fletcher, Abe and Charlotte, plus a BERT were all gathered for a critical assessment of the situation.

"Let us check," says Henri.

3 December

Action NASA

1   Full action test flight of the shuttle, Atlantis, Discovery, and Endeavour.
2   Certify pilots. One is doubtful.
3   Check the Europium is on target.
4   Propulsion, light drive.

Complete

4 December

Action Henri

1. Complete flight plans.
2. Send information and coordinate space and time to Zulu, Voyager and Belle Foret.

Complete

5 December
Action Fletcher

1. Issue the legal opinion of sabotage to Palma Systems.

Action Charlotte

2. Take Atlantis and the team to the space station to check the docking procedure.

Action IRIS

3. Perform checks with BERTS.

Complete

6 December
Action NASA

1. Still checking the Europium is on target.

Action Fletcher

1. Run the security checks on each person working on the project.

Complete

7 December
Action Fletcher and IRIS

1. Lock the shuttle site.

2.   Start the countdown 240,239,238, each item, location, every hour.

Complete

"Which brings us," said Henri, "to our next problem. I don't think the people of the other ships will be transferred to Voyager and Belle Foret. USS Independence, Arc Royal are ok, why abandon their ship?"

"Because of the degradation," says IRIS, "it is a time bomb."

"But we do not know if the Europium will fail," says Fletcher.

They were silent.

"Then," said Abe, "we must think again and quickly."

They were quiet for a moment.

"I propose that we meet here again at 15.00 hours with alternatives. The most critical is the Europium, we need a new source. Abe and Fletcher, please."

15.00 hours

"Abe, Fletcher?" Henri said.

"Well," said Abe, "it is now clear that we have been misinformed. There is another source in Malaysia with sufficient reserves."

"Why did we not know?" Henri said.

"Because the Saboteurs, Kostyantyn et al and the Anarchists Chopin, Bertrand, Gotier and Renard had modified the information. They deceived everyone."

"Bas*****."

"Vegetables," corrected IRIS

"When?" Henri said.

"February," said Abe.

Everything is quiet for a moment, no ticking clocks; they all exchange glances.

"Seems to me," said Fletcher, "that the risk is the same, stay, give up, go back, or go on."

Fletcher looked very comical as usual, blue hair, yellow nails and white overalls, but he had a very good point.

More silence.

Abe broke the silence.

"I suggest that we give all the facts immediately to the ships and wait for their decision. In the meantime, we continue for 17th. All in agreement?"

They all agree.

"That's it then, we're going for the 17th."

"Send the message."

The Spaceships, 12 December 19.40 Hours

All the bridges receive the message, it was short and precise. All the globes came on.

1 Stephanie Miller and Vincent Chu of Voyager, 2 Chih-Cheng of Lie-Long, 3 Abebe of Zulu, 4 Francoise la Blanc of Madame Juliet, 5 Brad Montgomery Independence, 6 Vladimir Sokolov of Vostov 4, 7 Fernanda Gomez of Belle Foret and 8 Aubry Elliott of Arc Royal 6.

"Well, that's quite just a message," said Vladimir.

"Yes," said Chi-Cheng, "but for the others, the choice is more difficult. On balance, I think the hazard is the return in consideration of the problems with the saboteurs and Europium."

"We have no problems," said Aubry.

"None here either," says Brad, "for us, it is better to go on and wait for the second mission in February."

"For us, February is too serious a problem," says Chih-Cheng, "it is touch and go."

"And," said Fernanda, "there is the problem of infrared degradation. This must be fixed or all ships will fail."

"It is a 2-way bet, 6 hours or 2 months," said Francoise, "what did Brad say?"

"We must ask everyone, a vote and then answer. After that, we will know which ships will go back and with how many people, and three ships are the maximum, including Zulu."

A ballot was prepared. "Answers by 13 December at 20 hours," said Abebe.

8 p.m., 13 December

The results were in. People are gathered around globes and screens on all the ships, in bars and restaurants, listening on headsets, in cargo areas, bridges and toilets, everywhere.

"Good evening everyone on all ships, I have the results of the votes," said Chih-Cheng. They are very interesting and a little surprising. Here we go.

All the bridges received the message, it was short and precise. All the globes came on.

1 Stephanie Miller and Vincent Chu of Voyager, 2 Chih-Cheng of Lie-Long, 3 Abebe of Zulu, 4 Francoise la Blanc of Madame Juliet, 5 Brad Montgomery Independence, 6 Vladimir Sokolov of Vostov 4, 7 Fernanda Gomez of Belle Foret and 8 Aubry Elliott of Arc Royal 6.

1. Zulu will be staying at the rendezvous position for the shuttle and then go to planet Earth.
2. Vostov 4 will be abandoned and transfer *7500 people
3. Voyager will be going on.
4. Belle Foret will go on.* and transfer 2000 people
5. Independence will go back to planet Earth.
6. Madame Juliet will go on.
7. Arc Royal 6 will go on.
8. Lie-Long will be abandoned and will transfer *8500 people

So only 27,800 will travel back to planet Earth at this time, the others will wait until February, and then decide.

23,300 will travel on Independence for a short time and can then be transferred to Zulu.

Right?

Okay, the message was sent.

Room 12, 14 December E at 02.30 Hours

Henri, IRIS, Fletcher, Abe and Charlotte, plus a BERT were all gathered to receive the fleet's message.

"Well," said Henri, "I did not expect that."

Fletcher was quick to comment, "The bottom line is that we must still go before February and we must have a solution to the infrared or they will all be dead."

"It's clear that they don't agree with the plan at the moment," said Abe, "and maybe they're right."

"In both cases, the risk is huge," says Charlotte. "We should re-examine the options for the infrared problem, so they could continue."

"Fletcher, please contact the White House and I will contact the fleet," said Abe.

From NASA at 02.35 Hours

"Michael? It's Fletcher. Sorry if I woke you up. I will be brief. We need a method to neutralise the infrared, it is not the screens, that's no good and we must have it by 30 January."

"That's all, money; no object. Good night."

Du Pont, 200 Powder Mill Rd. Wilmington from 07.00 hours. 14 December

Michael had called everyone together from the team.

Mary Bouchet, Technical Team Leader, Alexandre Jocovic, Logistics and Planning and Isabella Calvi second to the head of R&D.

Breakfast was on the credenza.

"Hello everyone, we have a new brief, there is no limit to spending and we must not fail. 30 January is the deadline. We need a new team and it can be worldwide. Back here at 12.00 hours with the list. Let's go."

ARC Royal 6 (1) 16 December

Aubry Elliott and the technical teams were busy making their arrangements before their return with the rescue team from Earth and before continuing with Voyager, Belle Foret and Madame Juliet. Gabriella had joined them and spent a lot of time on board as her relationship with Richard Thomas 1st Lieutenant had developed. As usual, Gabriella had a big cup of coffee, Meeka and her skates.

"The thing is," said Gabriella, "the rescue may not work, but if it does, we won't lose anything. Nothing ventured, nothing gained."

"Why is that?" Susan Baker, co-pilot says. "We would have failed."

"Because," says Aubry, "if we succeed here, the fact that we failed on Earth will not matter, we will still have an adventure mission."

The idea was to check if anyone wanted to travel back to planet Earth but other than that, it only remained to check the shuttle equipment before continuing the mission with Arc Royal 6, Madame Juliet, Voyager and Belle Foret.

Room 12, 17 December, 05.30 Hours

Charlotte, Fletcher, Henri, Abe, IRIS and a BERT, were all gathered for their final brief before their departure at 09.00 a.m.

"The news is that Dupont is close to solving the problem of infrared," says Fletcher, with a big smile and a flourish of his glasses.

"And," said Henri.

"And it involves polarising the shell with an electrometric charge that cycles in the same frequency as the infrared but it is pulsed at intervals of five minutes."

It seems to be working on the test but needs to be scaled up and it uses a load of energy, massive actually but it can be ready 20 January before schedule.

Endeavour 17 December 10.00 Hours

One hour into the journey, Charlotte and Henri were busy with the navigation. The bridge of Endeavour was narrow, the experience of travel at more than speed light, extraordinary, as it was before.

IRIS, Abe, Fletcher all stay on planet Earth.

"It's strange," said Charlotte, "how light-speed velocity changes our perception of the universe."

Briefly, Henri considers this.

"Yes, but far more strange is that we do not travel back in time as Einstein had predicted in his theory of general relativity. Then we could fix everything."

The BERT was busy making sure the cargo didn't move, Charlotte didn't have much to do and Henry began the countdown to briefings on an hourly basis to the fleet.

Endeavour, 30 Minutes Before Arrival at Zulu.

Henry had decided to stop at Zulu first, install the light drive, treat it as a dry run, then continue to the fleet and install the light drive in Independence. It was a good plan.

"20 minutes and counting," says Charlotte.

"10 minutes and counting."

"5 minutes and counting."

Henri and Charlotte studied the screens carefully.

60 seconds

50

20

And **10, 9, 8, 7 6 5 4, 3 2 1** and abandon the light-speed.

With complete horror, they had arrived at a field of debris.

Zulu 2 Minutes Before Endeavour Arrives

Mlungisi and Abebe had no time for action, all the screens were red, horns sounded, abandon ship...abandon ship...

The main spars of the two nacelles were broken and the body of the ship fractured from top to bottom which now is crushed by the free nacelles that carved through the atrium.

About 27 escape pods had succeeded but the rest were caught in the mayhem and were now twirling in space. There were bodies and body parts that rotated in space together with the broken parts of the ship.

Independence 17 December

Endeavour will arrive at 18:00 9 minutes 41 seconds after installing the light propulsion in Zulu.

-20 minutes and counting

-10 minutes and counting

-5 minutes and counting

-60 seconds

-50

-20

And **10, 9, 8, 7, 6, 5, 4, 3, 2, 1**

And there you have it...and?

Brad Montgomery and the team have been looking at the screens for the arrival of the Endeavour.

"It's late," Brad says to Ewan the co-pilot.

"It is impossible," says Brad.

"So where are they?"

"Give them 5 minutes."

Nothing.

"Send a message to see if they are still with Zulu."

"Okay," says Ewan.

Everything is quiet.

Ewan looks at Brad with a worried expression.

"Where are they?"

19 hours 51 minutes and 12 seconds

A blip of line, the screens go red...

"Independence? It's Endeavour, we're at the rendezvous with Zulu, it's a disaster, many deaths and wounded, the ship is in pieces. Hold your position and we will come for you. Endeavour out."

18 December

Delphine became accustomed to robots. The clicks were easy to understand and the history of the planet was very interesting.

The guard, George, was her constant companion.

There were changes in Delphine, she seemed stronger and her faculties improved, especially her sight and hearing and she was bigger.

Rupert 1 was a little worried. Five months to go before a possible rescue. Delphine was changed, maybe it will be too long.

Rupert decides a contact Oneson at Geodome 3.

Geodome 3

"Oneson," Rupert here, "we may have a serious problem. I think Delphine is evolving."

"What!"

"The ants are taking care of her and I think want to keep Delphine and therefore, they changed her."

"Are you serious?"

"Yes."

The Endeavour Shuttle

Charlotte and Henri were now working with the survivors. The plan is to gather everyone and then transfer them to Independence, which Charlotte and Henry hope to do soon.

It's now 23 hours 50 minutes 6 seconds on 19 December. In total, just 978 survivors of whom 120 are ok, 89 seriously injured and 29 walking injured. There are just 27 escape pods. A most pitiful number.

19 December

All the captains were gathered on Independence. Their plans have been drawn up.

-60 seconds

-50

-20

And **10, 9, 8, 7 6 5 4, 3 2 1 and there they are!**

Endeavour appears.

In 23 minutes, Henry, Charlotte (ex-Boomerang) and the BERT were on deck with, 1 Gabriella, Fletcher, Brad Montgomery (Independence)

2 Stephanie Miller, Abe Ito and Vincent Chu plus Randle Simms, Xaver Rhines, Bradley Hudson, Buzz Conke and Joe Ford all of (Voyager)

3 Chih-Cheng de Lie-Long 是志成 he is 29 years old and pilots the globe. Jaio-long 饶龙 (scaled dragon) is 31 years old, Li Jie 李杰 (beautiful hero); he is 26th very handsome and Jia Li 李佳

(Good and beautiful) and she is actually very beautiful and finally, Nuwa女岚 (creator of the whole universe); she is remarkably tall high and exceptionally beautiful, she is 27 years old.

4 Abebe and Mlungisi Manqoba of Zulu, 5 Francoise la Blanc of Madame Juliet, 6 Brad Montgomery Independence, 7 Vladimir Sokolov of Vostov 4, 8 Fernanda Gomez of Belle Foret and 9 Aubry Elliott of Arc Royal 6. (1)

"Hello everyone," says Gabriella, without skates but with coffee and Meeka as usual. "None of us thought that we would be in this situation when we began our journey, but here we are. The choices are very difficult, we have no guarantee that any of them will work. If we are all in agreement, Independence will return to planet Earth via Zulu, collect the survivors then in 6 hours 36 minutes and 41 seconds from now, fill up with Europium, gather the infrared team and equipment and return here by 20 January. We have to check if there are any who want to change their minds. We leave at 07.00 see you tomorrow."

There was silence then a cacophony of noise as everyone began to talk at the same time.

Start, 20 December

Eventually, there were 22,978 people, which included Zulu's survivors of 978, on Independence when it left. No problem, a short trip.

The return trip was quiet.

"Do you think that the whole saga was a mistake?" Gabriella said to Henri.

"Well, there was no choice and the Omniscient gave us none. If we return without incident, perhaps some will choose to stay on planet Earth. We'll see."

20 December 20 at 13 hours 36 minutes 41 seconds in the afternoon on Planet Earth.

"409,386,000 miles to go, 28 minutes 35 seconds until we pass the sun, then, 8.33 seconds and we are home," said Henri.

Geodome 3 20 December

Almost a month has passed, and Onesone's concerns are growing. Delphine is now speaking first by clicking, then in French.

Omniscient at the Same Time

1. Audry is very concerned for the survival of humanity. The fleet is decimated and Henri is a few minutes from disaster.
2. The balance of the fleet will be disintegrating without infrared protection. It must not happen.
3. On the Andromeda Galaxy, their chosen planet will soon begin to consume them all. Again.
4. I have to help them.

RECORD 8.

A figure is standing at a large 3-meter diameter globe that floats in a black space. The figure is spotted in colour, red and white with two arms and six digits per hand.

It has a large head, about one metre in diameter full of twinkling lights. A whirlwind of mist inside. There are characteristic similarities between IRIS and the cookies that demolished the buildings of planet Earth because of the appendages that appear from its sides and the recesses of about 150 mm around its middle. There is no surprise in this. There is no sense of a room, there are no edges, no walls or floor, it's just a space.

A screen appears on the globe. It looks like a library.

Along a shelf are a series of numbered spheres. The figure reaches for number 297. Suddenly, billions of images appear, names, places, events, times, galaxies, all scroll on the screens.

The tentacles scurry about and names appear.

1. Oneson
2. IRIS
3. Benton (Masahiko Takao)
4. Fletcher
5. Gabriella
6. Ludovic
7. Henri
8. Audry
9. Abe Ito
10. Mlungisi
11. Abebe
12. Delphine
13. Meeka (Gabriella's malamute dog)
14. Ruperts
15. BERTS

In this game, they are, or will be, the main actors. Of course, everyone is an actor but these are the favourites, and plus of course all the green eyes. He must keep all of those. And then there is Christophe Saint-Honore' and his beautiful, funny and MENSA-clever wife Tilda. French father; Danish mother. Only Henri knew what they did. They have a part yet to play. I like them.

The Omniscients however were not a good idea, not good at all and they will not appear again, particularly in **dimension 87. Complex of repairs.** Very, very annoying. They have to go.

The figure does not need to use its appendages but it is more pleasurable.

This game has existed for billions upon billions of years, but here, less than a day.

The animals and birds are a particular favourite, also all its creations in Andromeda particularly the silver ants. They will be useful again.

Insects and microbes too and the idea of free will, a masterstroke. The confusion of several languages is also very funny. But in reality, after 297 scenarios, enough is enough. He is done with this.

There is a disturbance behind the figure. A much larger presence enters the space.

It's difficult to determine how large or what its shape might be. It's more like a thought.

There is no colour, it is blacker than black, but with an occasional sparkle. Perhaps the sparkle is a galaxy, it's difficult to say.

"Hello, number 3 son."

"Hello, Dad, are you okay?"

"Very good, number 3, but really, you have spent too much time on this game. Tomorrow is another day, new games please."

"OK, Dad, just a few loose ends to tie up."

Son 3 had to remove Gabriella and Meeka from the globe place. I liked them a lot and their input to the globe and therefore the game was really good, lots of changes, very exciting.

"OK, no 3, get a wiggle on."

To Be Continued, Experiment No. 298. It Will Be Better.
298

Gabriella's Sketches

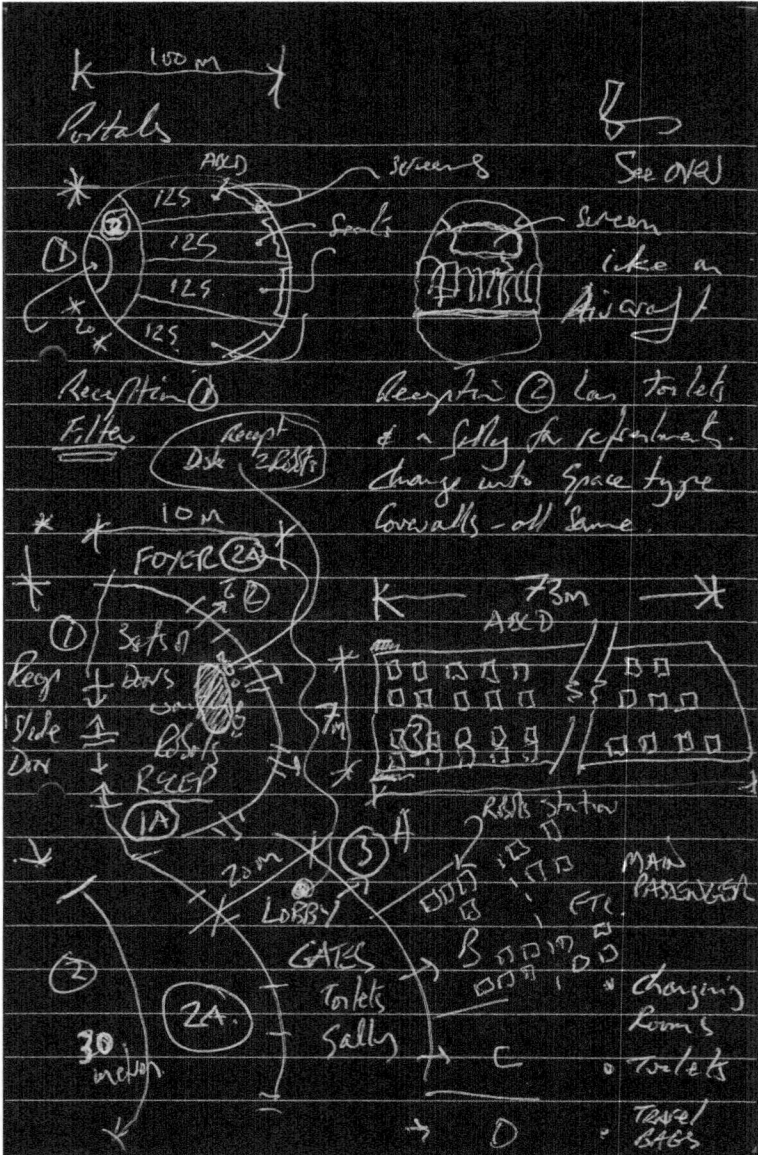

Portal: Departure Gate. Earth

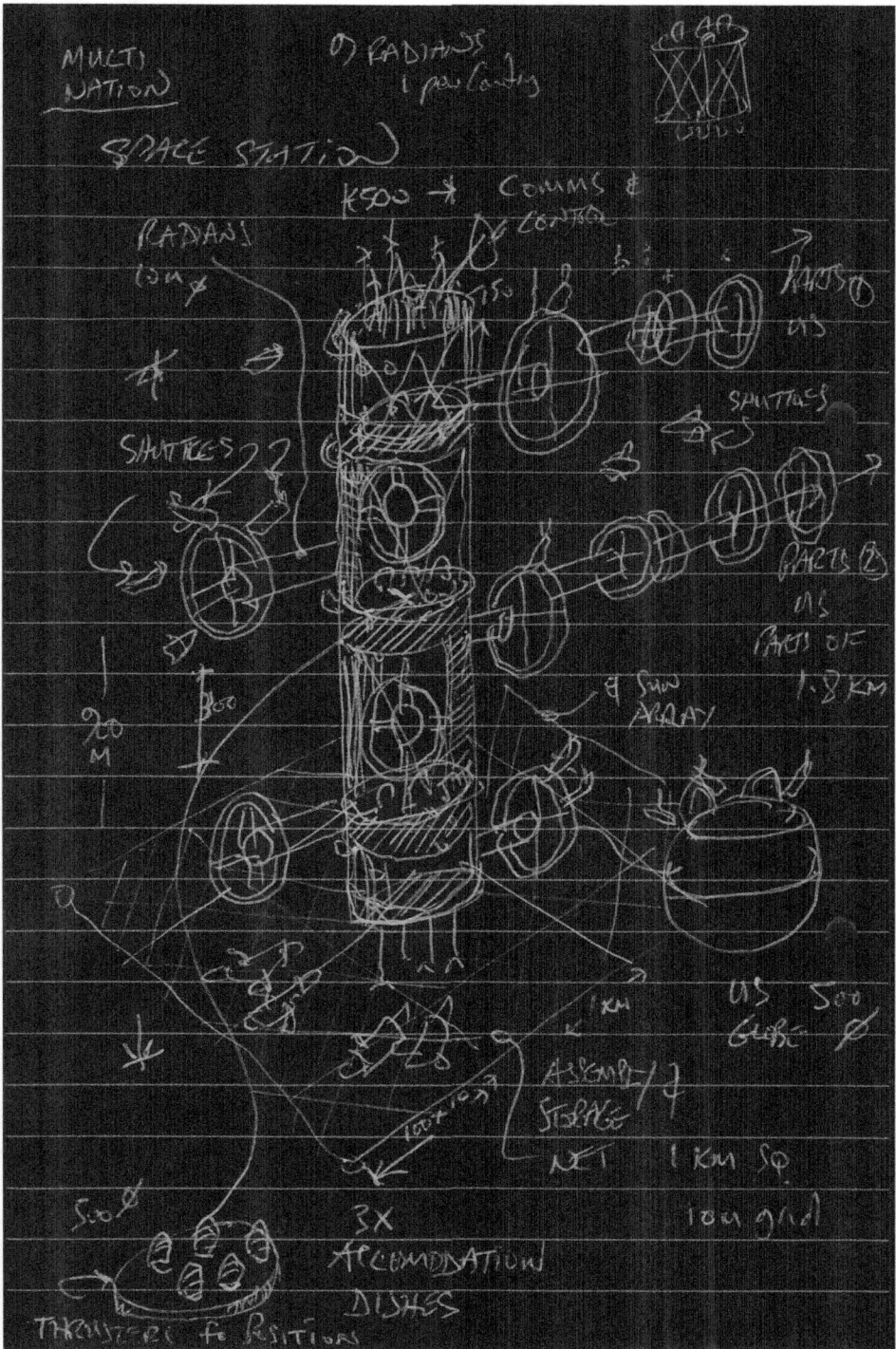

Space docking station . Earth

The cookies steal Manhattan. It begins

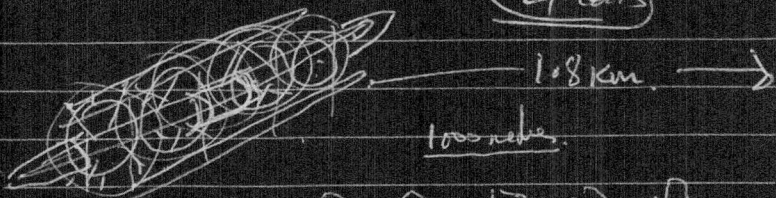

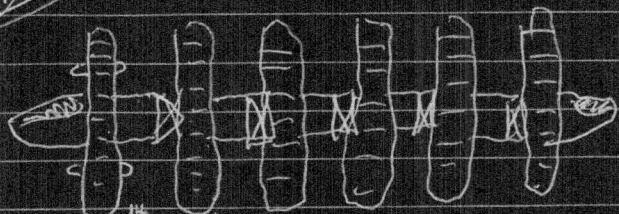

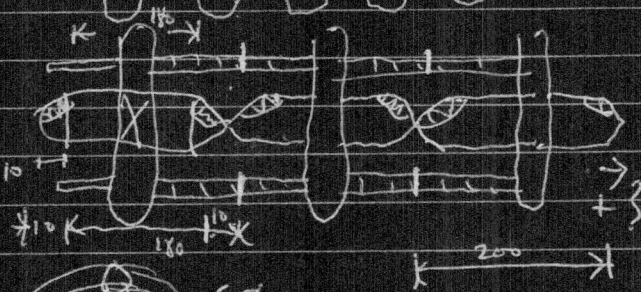

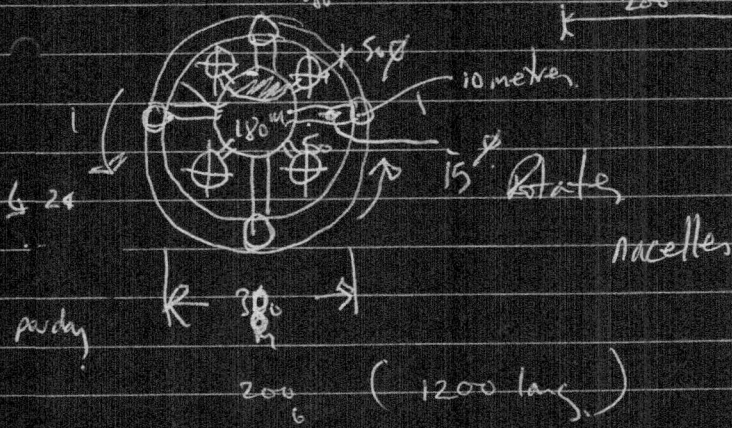

The American ship

3ft = 0.91 metres

✻ ⇒ Radius is approx 4,000 metres ✻

Revisit 1)

50,000 people in 5 domes

= 10,000 per dome - say, 3 floors

$= \frac{10000}{3} = 3,300$ per floor

@ 150 sqft per person

= 3,333 × 150 = 500,000 sqft

which is just one ~~~~~~~ per floor

(1 acre = 43,560 sqft)

✻ 10 Acres per floor ✻

in spare = 22,720 sqft

ATRIUM

150 sqft × 3333 per floor

core ~~~~~~~~

on

vertical access

radial access.

main access tube

ground level

100 metre candle

Earth Station Domes. They won't go there

Arc royal. British ship. A good ship

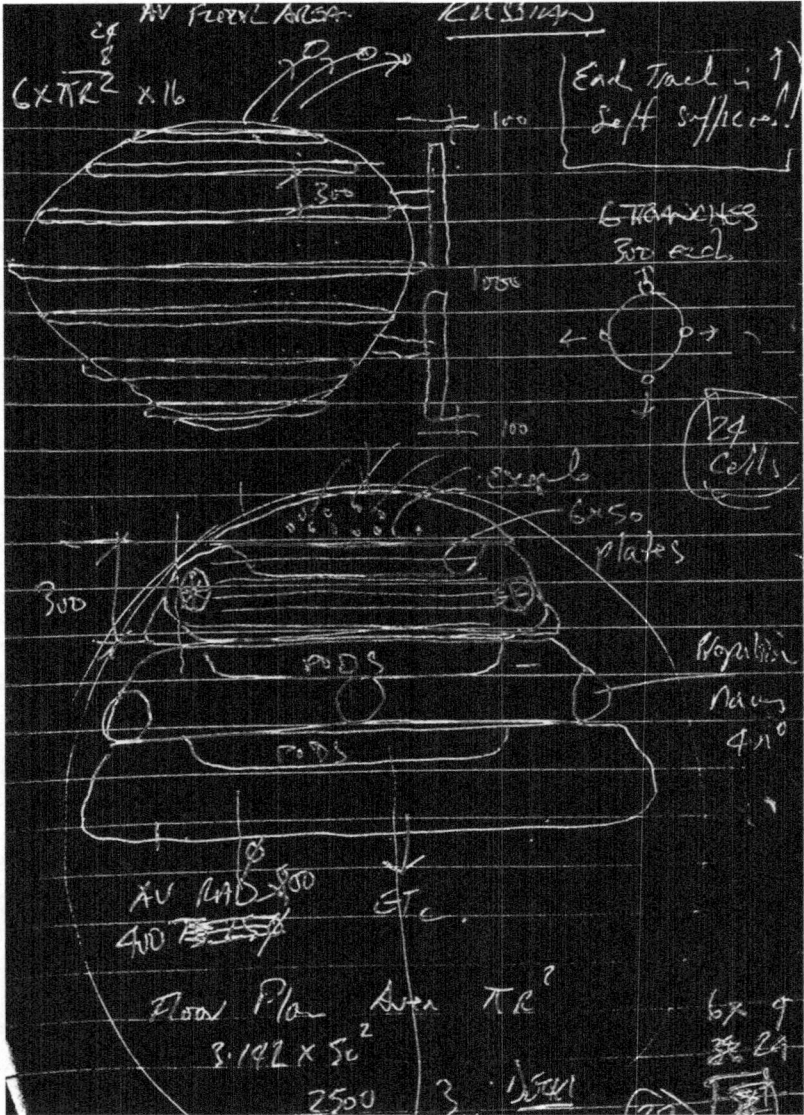

Vostov: The Russian Ship – the biggest of them all
Destined for Destruction

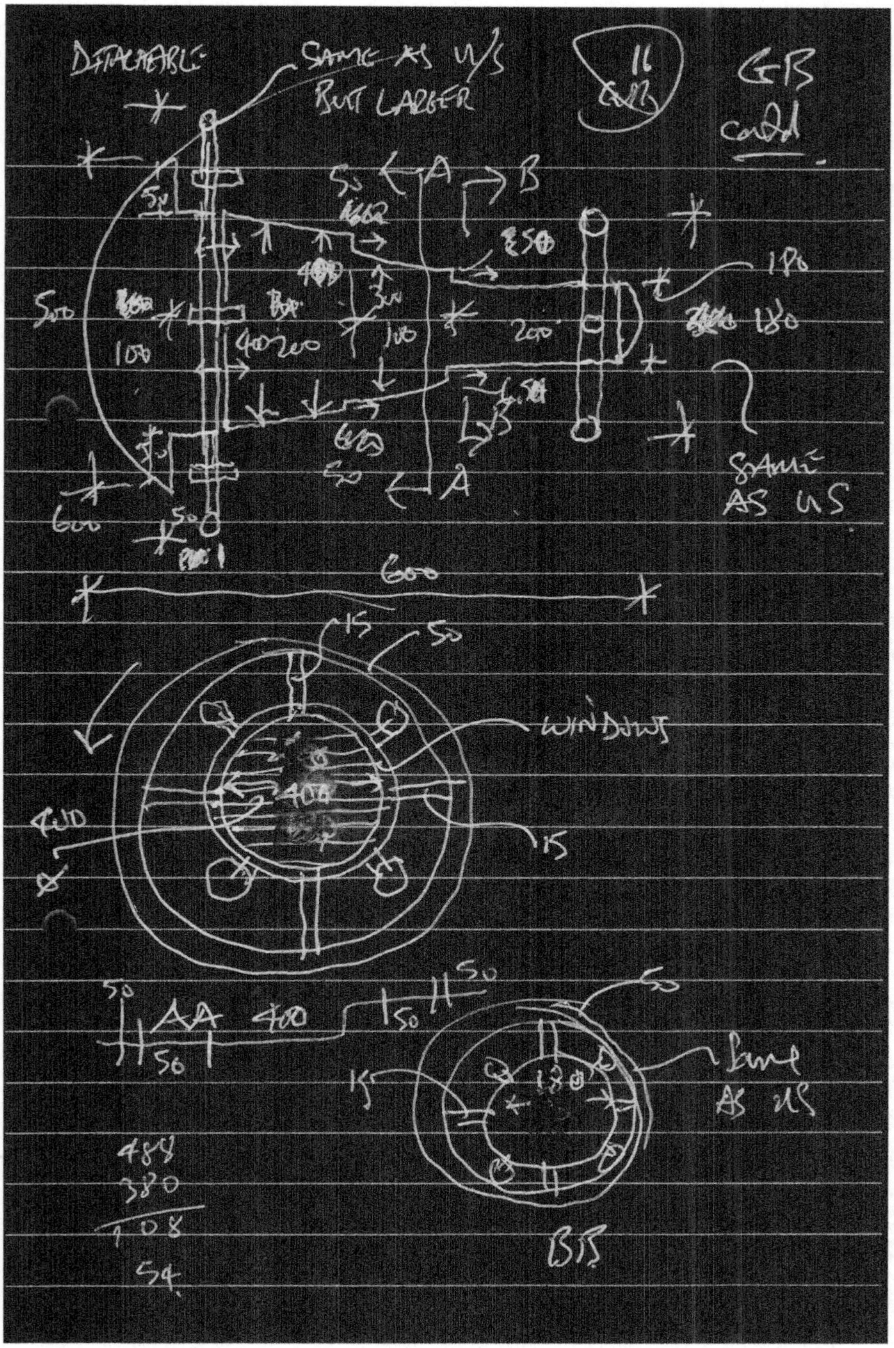

DETACHABLE

SAME AS U/S BUT LARGER

GB cont'd.

← A → B

500

180

200 180

SAME AS US.

600

600

15 50

WINDOWS

400

FWD

15

50 AA 400 50 50
50

15 180

Same AS US

488
380
108
54.

BB

Arc royal. decoupled

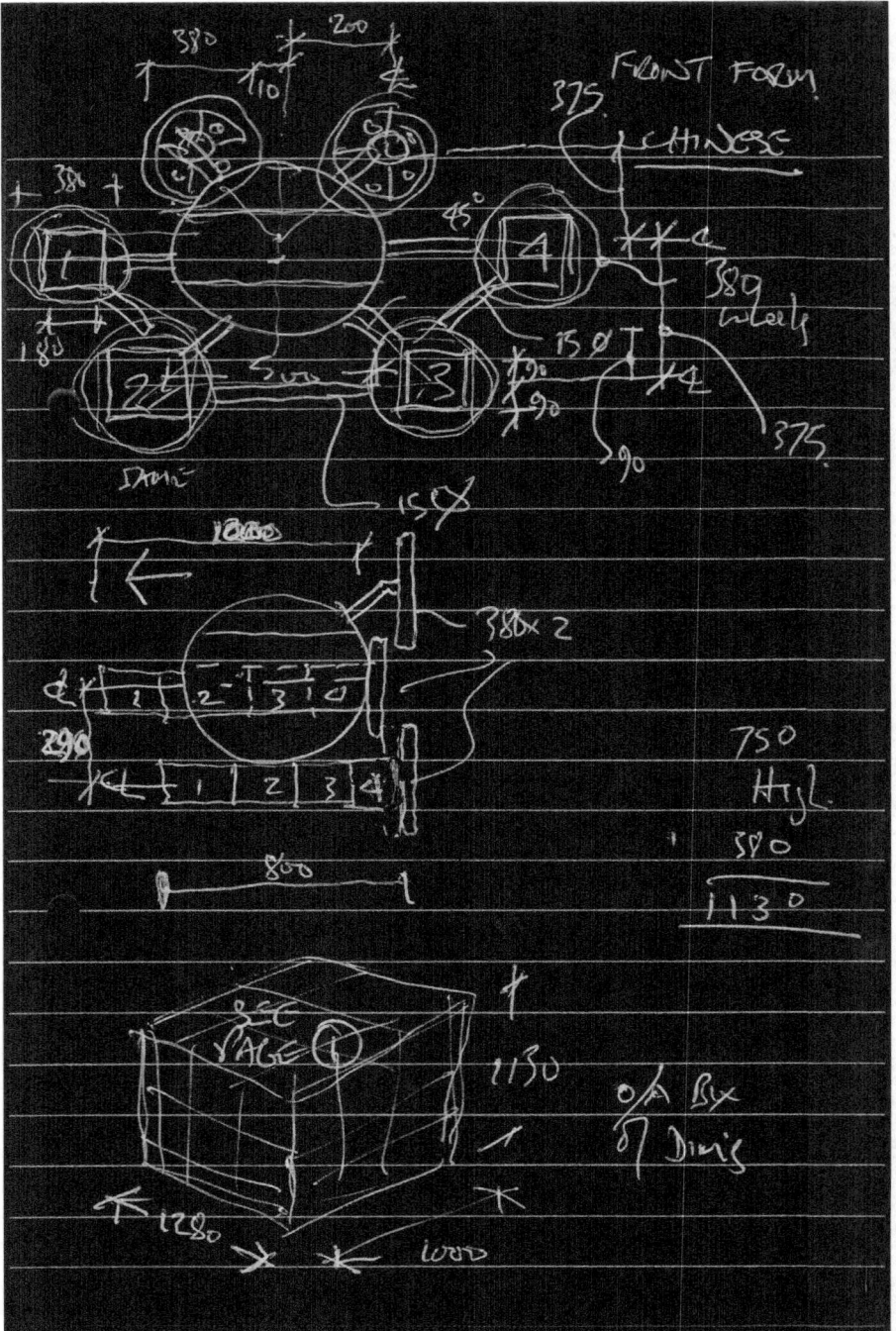

Chinese.The Aussie ship Boomerang is the same type. It does not survive

29 Cells

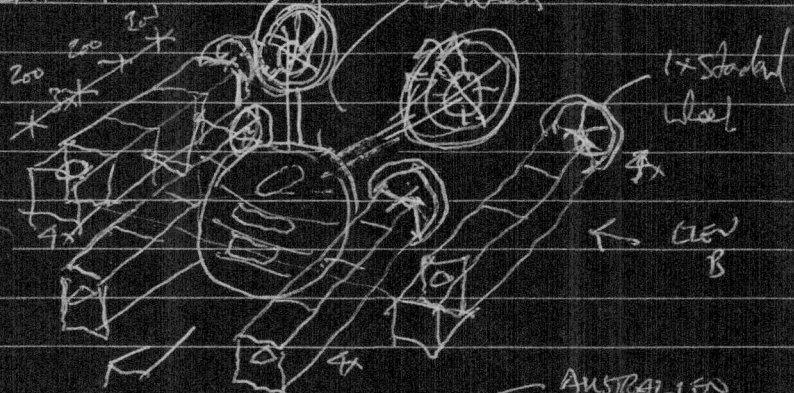

CHINA

2x Wheels

PAGE 1

1x Standard Wheel

CLEN B

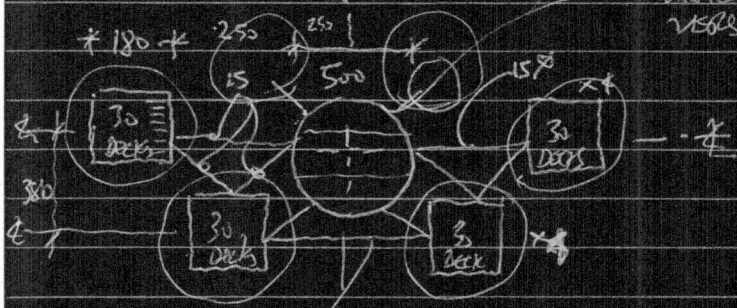

AUSTRALIEN VERSION

180 250 250
15 500 15
30 DECKS
300
30 DECKS
30 DECKS
3 DECK
3 DECK

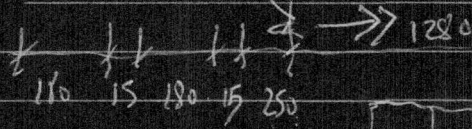

>> 1280

110 15 180 15 250

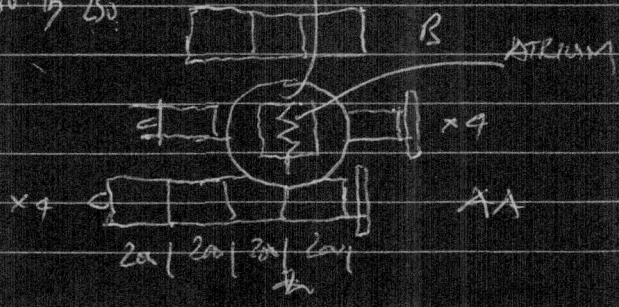

ATRIUM AS AUSTRALIA B

ATRIUM

x4

AA

20 | 20 | 20 | 20

Chinese

floor plate to

Slide say av.

200 ø 30

R = 200 × 8 bars

255   250

20 50

400

380 ø

250

185

180   90

1   2   3

200

380

K   600

20 50

phn steel

400

Sizes 200 × 180 × 30

4 × ~~180~~ × 30 each Main   4,320,000

× 4   17,280,000

Plus Slide

$\pi R^2 \times 80 = 3.142 \times 400^2 \times 80$ 40,217,600

S/m.   57,497,600

+ Webs + Gictube

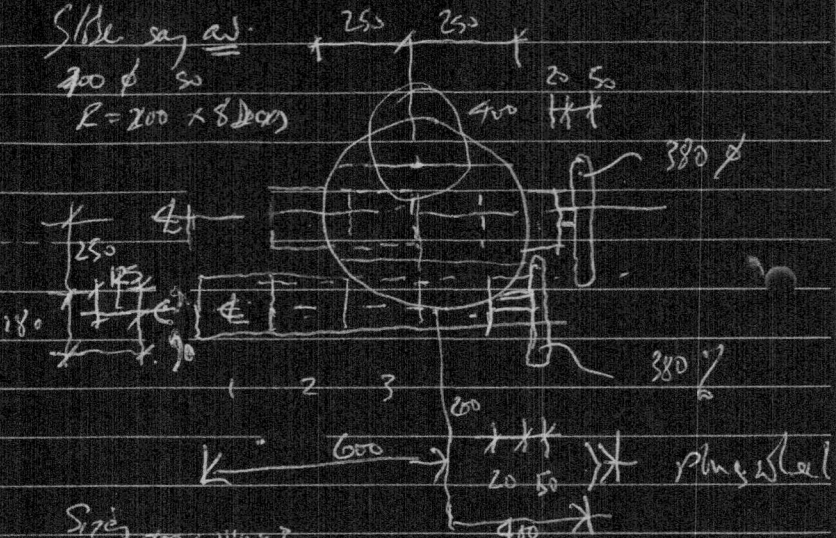

3g

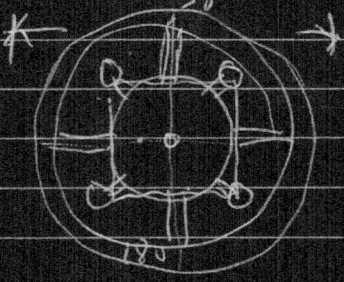

180

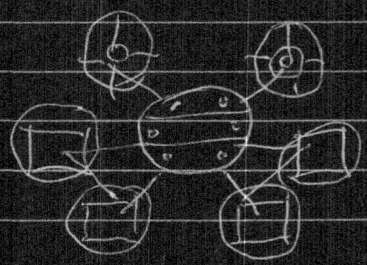

Chinese

French Ship. It's flamboyant

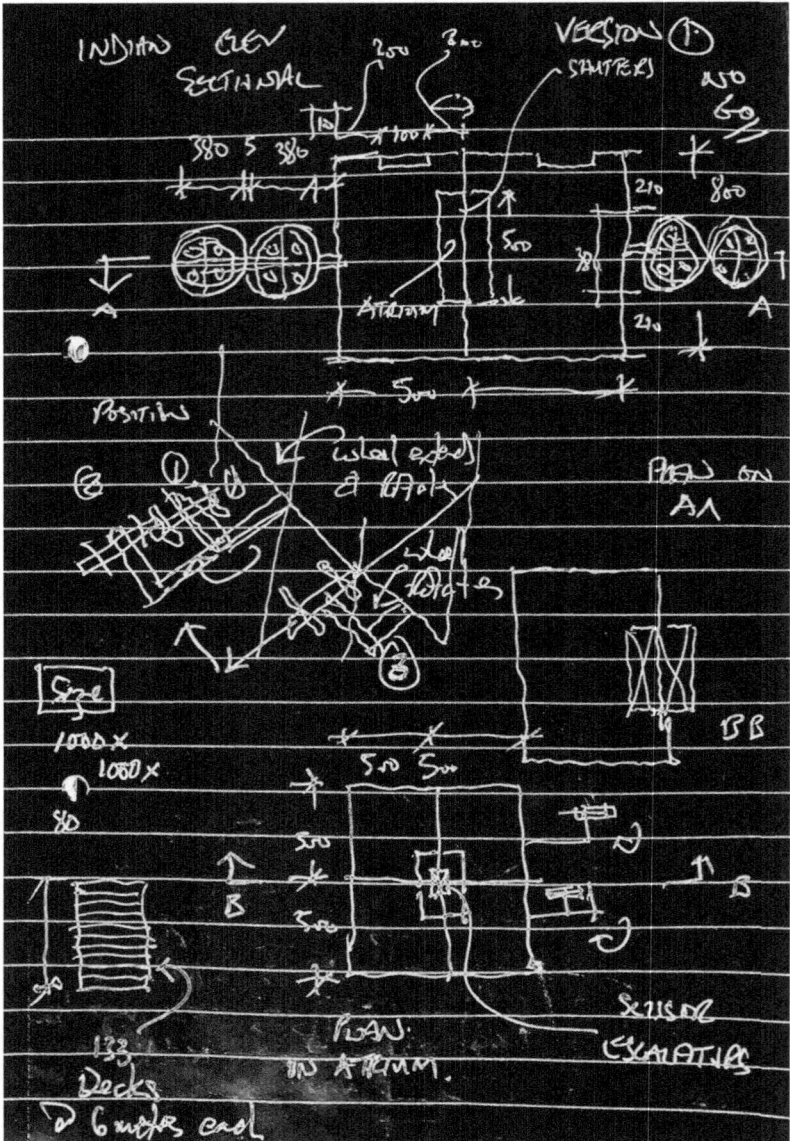

Indian design No.1 not be built

Indian Design 2. Not built

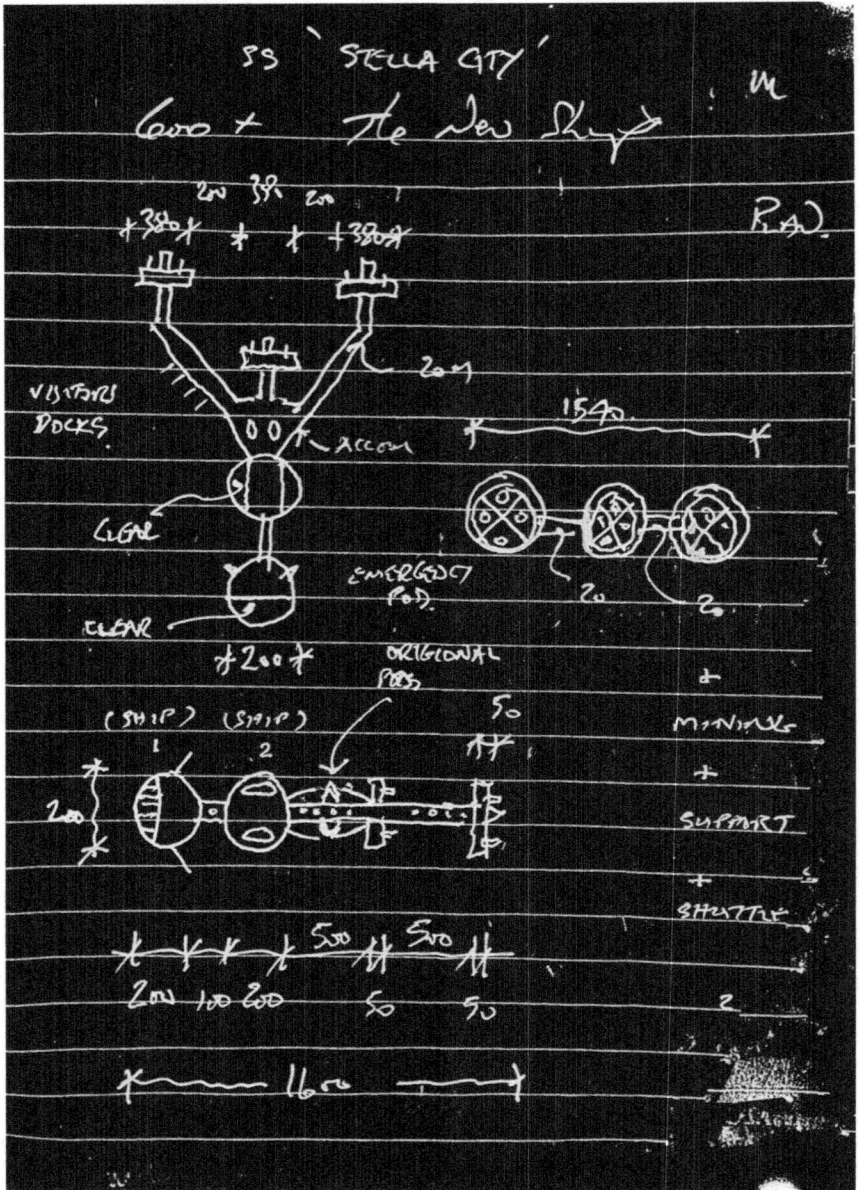

Stella City. Perhaps ,arises from the debris

2036 - Portal ready to go.
         Rupert disappears

2040 - Rupert Returns (0·0000389
         seconds later)

⦿ * now 1 year until onboard
   A being ready with all spaceships
   & 3 years before Cut off date

2040 - January 25 - the Space Station

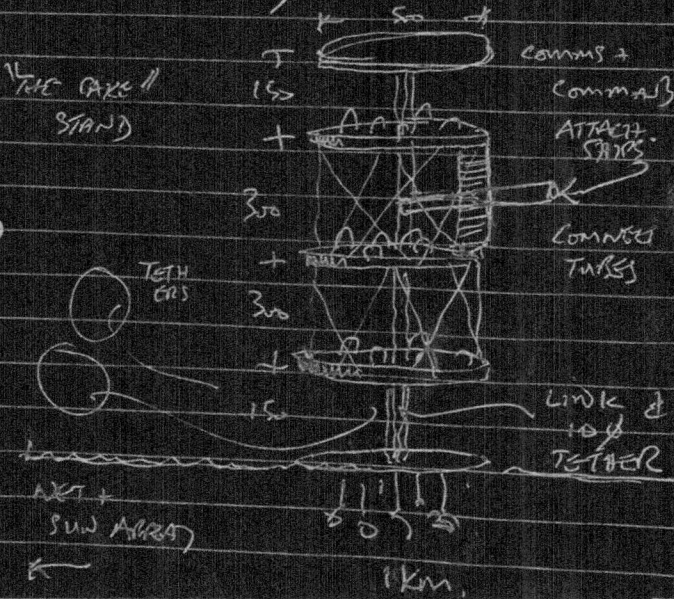

"THE CAKE "
STAND

COMMS +
COMMAND

ATTACH.
SHIPS.

COMMS
TUBES

TETH
ERS

LINK &
10 &
TETHER

ART +
SUN ARRAY

1 Km.

Docking Station

Andromeda `octopus' station has existed for millennia.
the silver ants are the guardians.
They will help in the next battle.
297 is not that battle

298

Printed in Great Britain
by Amazon

56246211R00110